CONTENTS

This book is dedicated to everyone who has helped me along the way. The people who have encouraged me to take chances and never look back. Those who have led by example, and those who have cheered by the sidelines, your gifts will never be forgotten.

ACKNOWLEDGEMENTS

I'd like to send a special note of appreciation to Emmanuel Comissiong, Rachael Lawrence and Mervita Welsh. Your input has been invaluable

CHAPTER 1

"Did you see that?"

Faye Morgan's head snapped around so quickly to look out of the car window that it resulted in an audible crack from her neck, but she hardly noticed. In fact, the only thing she'd really been noticing recently was the same thing that'd been causing her sleepless nights and making her question her mental stability.

"See what?" James Mason asked from his place in the back of the swiftly moving vehicle. He followed her gaze, moving back and forth trying to see...*something*.

"I don't know..." Faye hesitated. "It looked like..." she stopped again, not sure if she should tell them. Would they believe her? *She* hardly believed it herself.

"Looked like what?" This time it was Tony Anderson asking the same uncomfortable question.

He'd taken his eyes from the road to look at her. Faye saw something in his expression that offered a moment of comfort, but the realization of the last few days—*or was it weeks*—came flooding back and forced the feelings away.

She gave him a less than assuring smile. He was an experienced driver but she disliked it when he didn't pay attention while behind the wheel. Truth be known, Faye didn't like anyone not watching the road while driving, more so with a car filled with people, and as things were, she didn't need thoughts of an accident adding to her anxiety.

"I don't know," she repeated softly, nearly a whisper. "You guys will think I'm silly or overworked or something."

The day was bright and cloudless, but the sunlight couldn't pierce the darkness of her mood, which was like a storm threatening to wash away her sanity.

"No such thing," James quipped. "We know that you're silly and overworked, but the *something*...we're not too sure about."

Mason was the joker of the group and it was always good to have him along to lighten most situations, but at the moment she didn't appreciate his humour as much as she usually did.

"I just saw something that looked like..." once more her voice trailed off and a moment of silence took its place. "Never mind...I just thought I saw something."

"Well, I see something," James replied. "I see the guardrail, I see passing brush, I see trees zooming by. Hey, I think we might be in a car going somewhere."

It wasn't one of his better jokes, but it did confirm to Faye that she'd been right not to tell them after all. *I mean, who would believe me?* She asked herself as she turned to look back out of the passenger window.

Morose thoughts invaded her mind, tumbling through her brain like refuse from an upturned bin. *Am I going crazy? What's happening to me? Why is this happening? It can't be real...can it?*

It had started a few weeks ago, or maybe more—the events had created uncertainty within her—while she'd been driving to work. She'd thought she'd seen something, and though unsure of what it had been at first, the more she'd continued to see it out of the corner of her eye, the more recognizable it had become.

Convinced that she was overworked and in need of some rest and relaxation, Faye had asked her three closest friends to take a weekend trip to Diamond Beach. It was a five-hour drive from Concordia City, but well worth the ride if only to escape the bustling metropolis.

When they'd left, she had begun to feel more relaxed, knowing that for the remainder of the weekend, she would have her mind off of her work, her lack of a steady boyfriend, her disastrous finances and most of all, the death of her childhood friend, Nancy. Faye hoped that the weekend's campout would allow her to clear her mind and focus. Even though it had been less than a year since her last vacation—which was one of the issues overwhelming her at the moment—she'd still been feeling stressed and in need of another break.

In addition, she'd spent much more than she'd intended or could have readily afforded, but Nancy had really wanted to go to Italy, and hadn't wanted to go alone. Now she was dead and Faye had yet to come to terms with her loss.

The coroner had said that they hadn't found the cause of death, so had concluded that she'd simply died in her sleep. As a result of the lack of any injuries, her death certificate had stated *natural causes.*

At the viewing however, Faye had been certain that she'd known the reason. As she continued to look out of the window at the passing scenery, she drifted back to that horrible day at the funeral home. A shudder ran through her as memories of the events crept into her mind.

* * *

Faye arrived at the Mac Murrey Funeral home to be greeted by the sight of many people mired in different degrees of grief. Some wept openly while others maintained somber expressions on their faces. The opened coffin sat at the front of the room decked with flowers and surrounded by wreaths and mourners. She didn't need to see who was inside. On her way to the home, she'd been unable to stop thinking about how she would react to seeing her friend dead.

She looked around the room, but in truth didn't know why because she wasn't looking for anyone in particular. The entire thing seemed surreal, like walking in someone else's dream. With hesitant steps, she moved toward her deceased friend. Two ladies stood in front of the funerary box locked in conversation and blocking her view, so Faye waited in disbelief that she would never again share moments with Nancy.

It had been easy to ignore their conversation at first but gradually their words began to filter through her thoughts like a strengthening signal through static.

"She looks so peaceful," one of them said.

"Yes, she does," the other replied. "It's so sad when the young go so quickly."

"I know. But at least she didn't suffer. I think that going like she did is always the best."

Faye watched, still trying to get a grip on what had happened.

The first woman shook her head and continued, "I didn't even know that she was ill. I mean…Margaret never mentioned anything to me about her daughter being sick. Did you know that Nancy was sick?"

"No, I didn't. And as far as I know, she wasn't."

"What do you mean?" the woman gasped.

Faye nearly broke down. The words hit like a battering ram.

"Just that. As far as I know they couldn't find anything wrong with her. They just figured that she died in her sleep for some reason or other," the second woman replied.

She glimpsed the first woman's hand moving and guessed that she was making the sign of the crucifix. "Oh my God, that is so sad! I feel terrible for Margaret."

"Me too," the other agreed.

When they turned around, Faye thought she recognized one of them but wasn't sure. As the two ladies walked away still whispering to each other, her eyes trailed after them momentarily before turning to the coffin.

The sight that greeted her nearly knocked her to her knees in shock and disbelief. Nancy looked as though she'd been mauled by a wild animal. There were claw and bite marks all over her face and neck. Her throat had been ripped out and pieces of flesh hung in the creases of the wounds. One of her eyes dangled from its socket and her once beautiful red hair was matted and crusted with blood and brain tissue that had leaked from the track marks in her skull.

Faye was horrified and turned to leave, but stopped when she saw Nancy's mother approach the coffin with a wadded bunch of tissues in her hand. She used them to occasionally dab at her eyes and nose, both of which were red from crying and being wiped. Faye's heart went out to her, and for a moment she almost forgot that her friend appeared to have been viciously murdered and worse still, set out on display for everyone to see.

Their eyes met and Margaret burst into a fresh set of tears. Faye did the only thing she could think of and rushed to hug her in hopes of offering some comfort.

Margaret's voice shook but she managed to get the words out, "It's okay Faye, my baby's resting now."

Tears began to run down Faye's face as well, however, she wasn't sure if they were from the grief of losing her friend, or from seeing how she'd died. It was sickening that Nancy would be displayed in such a way. The undertaker should be fired and sued for what he'd done. And how could Margaret say that she was resting?

Faye felt her loosen her embrace so she released the other woman as well and watched as she turned back to her daughter.

"See, she's so peaceful," the grief-stricken woman said.

Her shock increased, "Who did this to her, Margaret?"

"It's God's will. I guess he wanted my angel back in heaven."

"But how did this happen?"

"I don't know, Faye."

Disbelief threatened to get the better of her, "No...really, Margaret, what happened to her?"

"No one knows, dear. No one knows."

"What do you mean? How—"

"I know, Honey. But they did an autopsy and couldn't find anything wrong with her. They couldn't find anything wrong with her. My baby just died...she just died," she sobbed and began to sag from her grief, so Faye reached out and held her again, then ushered her to one of the nearby chairs.

Her mind was awhirl. How could anyone think that Nancy had died in her sleep? How could they have done an autopsy and come back saying they couldn't find the cause of death? Had she been imagining things? Was the stress and grief of losing her friend taking a toll on her? How could she possibly have seen what she'd thought she'd seen? It had to have been her imagination.

With that resolve in mind, Faye determined to take another look. There was no way that they would have an open casket viewing if Nancy truly looked as she thought she looked. Further, it was highly unlikely for anyone else not to notice. She was sure that her mind had been playing tricks on her.

Slowly she turned from the grieving woman back to her dead friend. Her breath came at slow intervals as she tried to steady herself. Faye allowed her eyes to settle on the closed end of the coffin and work their way up almost of their own volition. They approached the floral arrangement positioned just before the opened end. There she forced them to pause while she fought for more control. When she was certain that she was prepared to see the truth, Faye allowed them to continue.

To her horror, nothing had changed. Her friend still carried the signs of an animal mauling; bloodied and torn, with her clothing in disarray. Some bones were even visible within the deep gashes that marred her chest.

She quickly turned away from the unnerving sight to look at Margaret again. The older woman sat in the chair nearly hyperventilating. Concern momentarily replaced the repulsion she was feeling so she looked around the room for something she could give the grieving mother that would help.

Spotting a table laden with bottled water and juices, Faye spoke softly to Margaret. "Lemme get you some water or something."

Not waiting for a reply, she began to walk towards the table just as an older man also began to approach the same area.

Faye recognized him immediately as Nancy's uncle Max, and remembered from the few times they'd met that he was a straightforward and forthright person. If anyone there would know what had truly happened to her friend, it would be him. He would also be the one to resolve the issue with the funeral home. Someone had to be held accountable for displaying her as they had, and she trusted that he would see to it. She was also positive that he wouldn't rest until the authorities had fully investigated the murder and found the party responsible.

Max noticed her and smiled. He was tall and thin and sported a goatee. Like his niece and sister, his hair was also red—what was left of it that hadn't turned grey or fallen out anyway. Despite that, it didn't take away from the fact that he'd probably been quite handsome when he'd been in his prime. From what Nancy had also said about him, he was wealthy, though he didn't seem to let it show.

"Hi, Faye. Thanks for coming. She always spoke highly of you," he embraced her and kissed her on both cheeks.

Faye didn't waste time on small talk. She wanted to know for certain that she was not losing her mind, "Max, what happened to her?"

"You know as much as I do. She died in her sleep."

She didn't try to hide her shock, "Max, do you think she died in her sleep? I mean...look at her," Faye gestured toward the coffin, "Does it look like she died in her sleep?"

Max shrugged, "That's how Margaret found her when she went to wake her up. They did an autopsy and everything came back negative."

"Autopsy? Did they even see her? They should be out looking for —"

"Out looking for what, Faye?" he gently interrupted her. "She was in her bed when she died."

The thought suddenly occurred to her that maybe he hadn't seen the body. It was possible that he'd arrived when Faye had seen him, and was only going on what he'd been told. Perhaps if he looked, then he would understand why she was finding it so hard to believe that Nancy had died in her sleep.

"Look at her, Max," she nearly pleaded. "Have you seen her?"

"Yes, Faye. I've seen her."

"And what did you see?"

"I saw my niece, Faye...dead."

"And?" she pressed.

"And what?" he replied. "She's dead."

"That's it? That's all you have to say?"

"What would you like me to say?"

She noticed that he was starting to become a little annoyed and although she didn't want to upset him further, Faye needed to find out what had really happened.

"I don't know, Max," she paused. "Anything...anything...like maybe you'll—"

"Maybe I'll what?" he didn't allow her to finish. "Maybe I'll pretend that she's not dead...that I'll pretend that she's just sleeping?"

"No...no..." she stammered. "I...I guess I'm just going crazy with the grief and the shock of it all."

She reached out to his shoulder and slid her hand down to his elbow. Faye then linked arms with him and led him to the coffin. Though she was still afraid of what she would see, she knew that it had to be done. A ray of hope that she would see her friend peaceful in death—as tragic as losing her was—flared within her like a pinprick of sunlight breaking through dark clouds. Faye had also been afraid that he would've resisted her attempts and was relieved when he'd allowed himself to be ushered to the coffin.

Unfortunately—but as expected—she still saw her friend's ravaged body. Stealing a glance at Max, she noticed that he was calmly looking at Nancy. Her instincts told her not to press the issue, but her distraught mind wouldn't let it go.

Her voice was small when she finally found it, like a child asking for permission, "Does this...does this look like sleep-death to you?"

He drew a breath and looked at her, making her think that she'd finally gotten through to him. When he spoke however, Faye couldn't miss the strain in his voice. "Actually, Faye, I don't know what sleep-death looks like, but if I had to guess, I would say yes. Yes, it does. Is there something wrong with you?"

That last rebuke finally shut her down, so reluctantly she let the matter lie. Perhaps it was somehow just her imagination; the stress of trying to cope with her current situation. "No...no, there's not. Sorry, I guess it's just the sadness of losing her...that's all. Sorry, Max...really."

He placed a hand on her shoulder, "It's okay. We're all a little upset right now."

* * *

"So are you going to tell us what you saw?" Maria placed a hand on Faye's shoulder, jolting her back to the moment.

"It was nothing. Just...something I thought I saw at the side of the road that's all."

It was best to leave it at that than to have to listen to James' sarcasm and the lack of belief from the rest of them. She also had to admit that she really couldn't blame them or anyone for not believing her because she was having a difficult time believing it herself.

The remainder of the drive was uneventful as was the weekend. On the trip home she didn't see anything strange or unnerving.

* * *

Faye awoke the next day feeling better. She'd fallen asleep as soon as she'd arrived home from the camping trip. The weekend getaway seemed to have worked wonders for her and she now felt that she could handle anything that came her way. She quickly showered and ate a light breakfast before leaving for the advertising agency where she worked.

In the middle of rush hour traffic with the music of Bon Jovi blasting from her car's stereo system, Faye felt relaxed. It was one of her favourite songs, and she couldn't help thinking that for once it was appropriate—in title at least if not in meaning. As the lyricists belted out the chorus *"Have a nice day,"* she smiled to herself knowing that she was finally going to for the first time in countless days...or weeks.

To her dismay however, she suddenly saw the same apparition that had been haunting her, and once again when she turned for a better look it retreated.

This weekend didn't solve anything, she told herself as her happy mood blew away like blossoms in a gale. She hated the thought, but Faye had to face the fact that there might actually be something wrong with her.

Maybe I should get help, she reasoned. There had to be a rational explanation for the things that were happening to her, and the sooner she resolved the issue, the better.

But what would my friends think if they found out? Faye could almost hear James' ridicule at her seeing a...*shrink*.

Would the others lose respect for me? What if it got back to the office? What would my co-workers think?

There were so many things to consider when faced with such a choice, but her alternative was equally as bleak. If she continued as she was, she might kill herself through lack of concentration, or an innocent person...maybe even a child. She knew that would be something that she could never forgive herself for.

The realization took hold like a suffocating fist. There truly was no other choice. *It won't mean that I'm crazy,* Faye assured herself, *it just means that I need a little help dealing with all the things in my life.*

She did her best to concentrate for the remainder of the drive to work. Her eyes focused on the road and her knuckles white from clutching the steering wheel. All the while the music on the stereo acted as a buffer between her and her thoughts.

* * *

Despite Faye's best efforts at the office she found it nearly impossible to get any work done. Her situation kept pulling at her like a carnival barker.

Finally deciding to put her resolution into action, she did an internet search for specialists, and on her first call was able to secure an appointment for the following day. The sightings continued sporadically; around the copy machine and then again in the kitchen when she reached for her fourth cup of coffee slightly before noon. The drive home took all of her focus as she struggled to stay between the dashed white lines. Her head snapped to the right frequently to catch a glimpse of something that would prove she wasn't completely losing her mind.

Faye's heart sank on one such occasion when she noticed that her experience with the apparition had changed. She didn't want to think of what it could mean so instead did her utmost to arrive home safely.

* * *

The following day it seemed to be at the corner of her eye more often than the previous weeks and an ominous feeling descended upon her. She'd no appetite and little desire to shower, but forced herself to do both. At least she was able to finish bathing, her distraction and fear made eating nearly impossible, so she gave up with more than half a bowl of cereal uneaten and her coffee untouched.

Not wanting to risk what would be a distracted drive into

work and then another to the psychiatrist, Faye called in sick. She told herself that she *was* sick. After all, there would really have to be something wrong for her to continue to see things that nobody else seemed to.

She tried to busy herself around her apartment rather than sitting worried, but after an excruciating hour and a half of fluttering, Faye decided to leave early for the appointment.

Upon arriving at the psychiatrist's—more than ninety minutes ahead of her scheduled time—she was greeted by a sight that made her stomach plunge as though she stood in an elevator to hell. The receptionist seated behind the frosted blue glass desk was bending forward examining something. From the top of her forehead which was visible through her red curls, Faye Morgan saw her friend Nancy. She could only gape as a mixture of shock, joy and disbelief rushed through her.

It can't be her, Faye thought to herself, *I went to her funeral. I saw her dead. I saw her buried.* The notion of it being a twin, or a biological sister surfaced in her mind, but she dismissed it because she knew that her friend only had a brother.

With halting steps she approached the desk; almost afraid to make a sound for fear that the secretary would raise her head and spoil the illusion...or worse, confirm it. She continued her pace until she stood over the other woman—who seemed oblivious to her presence as she rummaged around under folders. When she could stand the suspense no longer, she cleared her throat, causing the receptionist to look up at her with files in hand, and the illusion to vanish.

Though her hair was red like her deceased friend's, that was where most of the similarities ended. The lady before her was slightly older and lacked the same warmth in her eyes and smile.

Despite that, Faye couldn't dispel the notion of Nancy. Even when the other woman spoke, she heard her friend's voice in her mind.

"May I help you?"

Faye was transfixed by her own imagination. The words bounced off unnoticed as though they held no meaning. Eventually the expression on the receptionist's face brought her back to reality, and it took some effort for her to clear her thoughts.

Finding herself a little embarrassed, she smiled. "I'm...I'm Faye Morgan. I umm...I have an appointment with Dr. Dillington."

The secretary set the files to one side of the desk and tapped a few keys on her keyboard. She then read the screen and looked at Faye with a pleasant expression on her face. "You're quite early, Miss Morgan. The doctor is currently with another patient. Would you like to take a seat and wait or would you like to come back a little later?"

Images of Nancy looking at and speaking to her clouded her mind and were superimposed onto the receptionist by her fragile psyche. It took tremendous will for Faye to pull herself back again from the fantasy she'd drifted into, but her immergence had been too deep and she couldn't remember what had been said. She searched her mind but all she could find was the vision of her friend staring at her and moving her lips.

Realizing that Faye hadn't been paying attention, the receptionist repeated her question. This time the information made its way through and she decided to wait at the office. If she'd chosen to return later, and continued to be distracted by the apparition—and now her hallucinations of her dead friend—there was a possibility that she would miss her appointment.

Taking a seat on a black leather couch in a corner of the office, Faye began to absent-mindedly peruse a magazine. When her time arrived, she looked up to see the secretary standing in front of her with her hand outstretched. The puzzled look on her face was enough for the lady to realize that she'd not completed the questionnaire she'd been given. A slight embarrassment washed over Faye again when she noticed the other woman visibly restrain herself. She was advised that the form needed to be completed before she could be admitted to see the doctor. Faye had to really concentrate in order to remember even having been given the clipboard and document. When it was completed at last, she was ushered in to see the psychiatrist. The receptionist handed him the clipboard and left the room, closing the door gently on her way out.

Faye stared at the closed door before hesitantly turning her attention to the doctor and his office. He was *not* as she'd expected. When she'd played the scene in her mind she'd pictured him as an older graying gentleman with large-framed glasses and a polka dotted bow tie. He'd be either seated behind a large brown desk or directly beside a white leather couch. She had envisioned a wood-paneled office adorned with numerous credentials from all of the most famous institutions.

It was a surprise to see that the doctor did not seem to be much older than her own twenty-nine years of age. In place of the paneled walls was a neatly painted blue room. The credentials *were* there of course, though not nearly as many as she'd thought. In fact, there was only one. Instead of a large brown desk, a variety of chairs were arrayed around the room—two in particular sat on opposite sides of a stylish coffee table. She also couldn't help noticing his magnificent green eyes, and instantly found him attractive. This helped to ease her anxiety a little—at least about seeing a *shrink*, anyway.

"Ah Miss Morgan, have a seat," he said, not indicating anywhere in particular.

Most of the trepidation that had remained fled after hearing the rich seductive tone from the handsome man. A part of her began to regret that they were meeting under such circumstances. Had the situation been different, Faye was certain that she would have tried to flirt with him—though she'd never been very good at it. Focusing back on the moment, she chose one of the chairs at the coffee table, the doctor took the other.

"Now, before we begin, I just have a few additional questions. Some people don't feel comfortable knowing that someone other than their doctor might read their information," the psychiatrist said as he looked from Faye to the clipboard and back again. She nodded so he continued, "How old are you, Miss Morgan—if you don't mind my asking?"

"That's okay. I'm 29," Faye replied.

He made a note on the document, "Have you ever seen a psychiatrist before?"

"No."

"Are you currently taking any medication that I should know about?"

"No," Faye repeated the single word answer and her desire to flirt melted like wax in a flame. The reality of where she was and why reasserted itself and her mood became timid.

"Okay then, the rest we can tend to later. So...why don't you tell me about what brings you here today," he said.

She took a deep breath, "I think there's something wrong with me."

Instantly she realized how it might sound to a psychiatrist but as with all thoughtless speech, it was too late to retract the words. His raising of an eyebrow confirmed that she'd been correct, so she tried to cover her embarrassment with a little cough.

"It's okay, Miss Morgan. I understand. Most people are a little nervous when visiting someone of my profession for the first time," Doctor Dillington reassured her.

She wasn't certain how to respond so she simply stared at her hands. Visions of her friend streamed through her mind and she tried to steady her breathing as her revulsion began to rise. It was fortunate for her that the apparition also chose not to appear—or perhaps her mind chose not to make it appear.

"Please…continue when you're ready," he informed her as the silence stretched.

After a few more moments of hesitation she resumed, "As I'd said, I think there's something wrong with me."

"That might be a very harsh description. What makes you say that?"

"I think I've been hallucinating."

"You think…or you have been?" the doctor asked.

Faye stammered, "Well, I…I…"

She'd picked up what she thought was sarcasm in his remark and began to wonder if he were trying to make fun of her. However, she quickly realized the absurdity of the notion. He was a professional dedicated to helping people deal with issues in their lives. It was unlikely that he would attempt to ridicule or belittle them. This was definitely more proof of her overactive imagination getting the better of her. In much the same way that she'd imagined his secretary as Nancy.

Knowing this offered little solace and made her wonder if maybe she'd been a too hasty in deciding to see a psychiatrist. After all, if she knew that it was her imagination, then she should be able to deal with the issue on her own.

"Please try to relax, Miss Morgan. My job is not to judge, but to offer assistance."

Faye breathed deeply again. Although his words were meant to be reassuring, they only served to prolong her inner conflict and doubt regarding her visit. Perhaps it *was* just the stress of her disastrous life recently that was the cause of what was happening to her. The things she'd been seeing couldn't possibly be real.

"Okay," she tried again. "I *have* been hallucinating. But I think that…I mean…I'm sure that it's only because of all of the stress I've been under lately."

Faye couldn't read the look on his face, but she prayed that his thoughts were nonjudgmental.

"When you say hallucinating, what exactly have you been seeing?" he asked

"Well…" she paused and decided not to tell him about seeing Nancy when she'd first arrived. "It looks kinda like…kinda like a claw. At first it was only at the corner of my eye, and every time I tried to get a better look, it always vanished. I should say it *had* always vanished. Now it's changed, it seems to be staying longer and…"

"And?" he prompted.

"And…it seems to be getting closer."

"Can you describe it to me—I mean…what…kind of *claw* is it?" the doctor asked.

"It's green and reptilian looking with really sharp nails. I can see it, and I can see the arm but nothing more."

"Hmm," he replied. "Tell me, have you undergone any stressful or unusual events recently that you've not mentioned?"

"Well," Faye paused.

She thought about lying, or maybe omitting what she'd seen at the funeral home. What would he think if she really told him everything? Would he have her committed? Maybe placed under suicide watch? What would her friends say about that when they found out? So many different scenarios played with her mind. Finally Faye decided that if she wanted help, *truly* wanted help, then she would have to tell him everything, again with the exception of what had happened earlier.

Steeling herself she proceeded, but not without a bit of caution, "My long-time friend Nancy was buried a couple of weeks ago...and..."

"Go on."

"At the viewing..."

Faye cast her eyes to the floor and shuddered as she recalled the damage inflicted to her friend. The bones protruding through the flesh of her shoulder, the brain matter that had seeped through the slashes in her skull, her dangling eye, her opened throat. Those images sent a shock through her as though she'd fallen into an icy lake. The thought of it made her bile rise, and with effort she forced such scenes from her mind so she could continue.

Risking a glance at the doctor, she noted the calm demeanor with which he was regarding her. She didn't want to associate his look with skepticism but couldn't help it, and in some ways, couldn't blame him. In the back of her mind however, she prayed that he would believe her.

"What of it?" he prodded.

"That's just it...it was weird."

"In what way?"

"The body...it was...it was *hacked* to pieces," Faye could

barely force the words out and the memory caused her to begin to sob and search her purse for a tissue.

Dillington reached under the coffee table and placed a box of Kleenex within her reach. She pulled two and dabbed at her eyes and nose before thanking him.

"I don't understand Miss Morgan. If the body was…*hacked*… to pieces, they wouldn't have had an open casket viewing."

"I know…I know, but they did. And worst, no one seemed to notice. They were saying they couldn't find the cause of death. That she simply died in her sleep. Everyone was commenting on how peaceful she looked. It was like they didn't see it."

"Mmm hmm."

She was dismayed, "How could they not? Were they blind?"

"Tell me Miss Morgan—"

"Please, Faye," she sobbed. Though she was distraught, the term *Miss Morgan* seemed patronizing.

"Okay. Tell me Faye, were you seeing this…*claw* before or after this situation?" he asked.

She thought for a moment. "I'm not really sure. I think it may have been after, but I can't really say because everything lately has seemed so surreal…almost like a blur."

"Indeed, I can only imagine. But still…very interesting." At her quizzical look he continued. "I'll explain in a moment. How has your sleep been prior to and following this tragedy?"

"Well, as I've said, I've been under a lot of stress lately, and I haven't been really sleeping well."

"Hmmm…anything else?"

"I've also made a complete mess of my finances. It's so bad that I'm barely making it by month to month. And…"

"And?"

"And…well, I've been kinda lonely lately. I haven't had a steady boyfriend for a long time now, and I kinda think a lot about both almost every night, so it's sometimes hard to quiet my mind and get to sleep"

"I see," he said. "Let's go back for a moment, if you don't mind."

"That's fine Doctor."

He smiled, "Thank you. But before we begin however, please understand that these questions are not meant to pry, per se, I'm just trying to determine how best to help you."

Surprisingly, his words offered Faye a ray of comfort and allowed her to drop the defensive barrier she'd unknowingly erected. She finally felt that she was indeed doing the right thing in seeing a psychiatrist. With that realization, relief washed over her like a rush of warm air.

"It's okay Doctor Dillington. That's why I'm here."

"That's very good to hear you say that Faye. Being open to the nature of the help is the only way to ensure that we are truly helped. Now, as I was saying. You'd said that you'd made a mess of your finances. Do you mind if I ask how exactly you've managed to do that?"

Although she'd become comfortable talking to him about her mental state, that didn't extend to her financial well-being. Regardless, she did her best not to feel embarrassed by her situation. "Well, among other things, I took a trip that I really couldn't afford with my best friend Nancy."

"Is she the one who unfortunately was buried a short time ago?"

"Yes."

"I understand—and my condolences, by the way—but may I

ask where you went on your trip?"

"We went to Italy," she smiled as the memories of her vacation brought her spirits up a little.

"Interesting, but Italy can be done on a budget. I went backpacking there myself when I was in university. Either way, how exactly did you exceed your limit? Did you stay at expensive hotels...or maybe you ate at expensive restaurants? I can certainly understand the temptation because Italian food can be quite delicious after all."

"Yes, it is delicious, but we did our best to do the trip on a shoestring budget. We ate at little cafes instead of restaurants. We even slept at the Abbey Starita for one night."

Dillington raised an eyebrow, "Oh? How did you manage that?"

"One of my coworkers is Italian and he recommended it to me when he found out that I was going to be visiting his country for three weeks."

"Well, that was very nice of him. Why did you only stay at the abbey for one night? I can't imagine that they would have charged you a lot to stay longer, if in fact they charged you anything at all."

"Well, that's a long story," she answered a little sheepishly. "But unfortunately, we weren't able to stay longer. Also, since most of the hostels were booked, we had to stay at hotels sometimes. And yes, some of them were beyond my budget, but we didn't really have much of a choice. I guess in many ways, we didn't plan the trip very well."

His response was quick, "Yes, I can imagine...if you exceeded your budget."

Realizing how it would sound but unable to stop herself, she decided to go further. *Might as well get everything out in the open,* "I also spent a lot of money on first class tickets for the trip."

"Really? Do you always fly first class?"

Faye tried to hide her embarrassment, "No...no...we—I don't...and I don't know why we did this time either."

"Why do you think you did?"

"Honestly...I really don't know. Maybe we both just wanted to go so badly. And as stupid as it may sound now, at the time that we booked the tickets we really didn't care about paying the extra cost."

He shrugged, "Well, in some ways the important thing is that you both enjoyed your time there. You *did* enjoy your time there...didn't you?"

"Oh, definitely."

"That's good. Maybe I'll take a trip there myself sometime in the near future. Sorry...you'd just brought back some memories. But you had also mentioned feelings of loneliness that sometimes keep you awake?"

"Sometimes," Faye responded.

"What about your dreams—when you *are* able to sleep?"

"I've not...I don't think I've been having dreams."

"Hmm, that's not good. The body needs sound sleep. REM sleep. If you're not dreaming then you're not entering that phase. Without it the mind begins to break down and we start to hallucinate. I'm going to recommend some sleeping pills for you." She started to object but he raised a hand to forestall. "Don't worry they'll not be addictive. They're just so you can sleep, and most importantly, dream.

"Overall, I think it's your subconscious mind reacting to being deprived of much needed rejuvenation as well as your recent loss. The claw could be representational of something ripping away what seemed to have been a bright spot in your life. A foundation...if you will, namely your...*childhood*...?" Faye nodded, "Your childhood friend.

"The next time you see this...claw, I want you to concentrate on it and try to determine what it and the arm are attached to. Once you can confirm that there is nothing there, your mind will realize that it had hallucinated all the events and it will begin to heal itself—the human mind can be a very resilient thing—and the apparitions will fade. I think we should schedule follow-up sessions, if you will, so we can further try to get to the core of what's troubling you."

The doctor scribbled a prescription onto a medical pad, tore off the note and handed it to Faye. "My secretary Lauren will help you with further appointments."

Faye accepted the slip and thanked him. On her way out of his office she stopped by the reception desk and forced herself not to think of Nancy when she saw the woman behind it. She found that making the follow-up appointment was not as embarrassing as she'd feared. In fact speaking to Lauren was easier when she refused to allow her mind to associate her with her friend.

Although the initial appointment had been brief—she'd originally thought that it would have been a longer session—she felt certain that the worst was behind her.

That night with the help of the medication she slept better than she had in a long while. The following dawn, she awoke felling very refreshed and confident that the day ahead would be a good one. On the drive into her office, the vision came again and as usual vanished before she could get a good look at it. The second time she saw it however, she didn't look over as quickly. Since she hated drivers taking their eyes from the road, Faye resisted the urge until she arrived at a stop light. After several deep breaths she tried the doctor's suggestion and concentrated on moving the image from her periphery to her main vision.

Then she realized, but it was too late, the demon was upon her. Razor sharp talons started to hack and slash at her face, breasts, and throat. She raised her arms in an attempt to ward off the blows but soon they too were torn to shreds. In her desperate struggles, her foot slipped from the brake to the accelerator and the vehicle sped through the intersection. Faye hardly noticed as she was in a fight for her life. Her car rocked from the momentum of the battle as the thing viciously mauled her. The last things she heard were her own agonized screams and the crunching sound of metal on metal.

* * *

"I can't believe she's gone," Maria whispered, her voice was heavy with grief and she dabbed at her eyes once again.

The three friends, Tony, Maria, and James stood beside Faye's opened coffin. The room in the funeral home was filled with a variety of wreaths, floral arrangements and mourners.

"I know, it's tough," Tony replied as he momentarily put his arm around her in comfort.

"What the fuck happened to her?" James demanded slightly above a respectable whisper.

"Hey, c'mon show some class," Maria admonished him. "It was the damn airbag. It's supposed to be a safety feature but the damn thing killed her."

"Airbag?" he whispered back, once again a little louder than he'd intended. "Airbag...she looks like she hit a fucking industrial harvester. What the fuck is wrong you. What the fuck is wrong with all of them?" he indicated the other mourners with a wave of his hand.

"Keep your voice down and show some tact," Tony repeated Maria's reprimand. "She looks fine...all things considered.

James couldn't reply because the revulsion of seeing the claw marks all over Faye's face and visible body momentarily silenced him. He knew he should turn away from the gruesome scene but his morbid sense of curiosity kept his attention riveted. Some of her injuries were still fresh even though she'd been killed a week prior. They glistened and dripped onto the fabric of her coffin. The parts of her brain visible through the troughs that had been dug into her skull reminded him of cauliflower.

At last he found his voice, "She doesn't look fine, she looks like shit!"

Maria burst into tears anew, but even that did little to taper his disgust. Tony put his arm around her shoulder again and glared at him, "You know...you can be a real asshole sometimes, you know that."

With that, he led her away from the confrontation. James turned to follow but stopped, because out of the corner of his eye, he saw it.

CHAPTER 2

"Are you sure?" Nancy Carman yelled to make her voice heard above the raging wind.

"Yes. Trust me Nance," Faye replied. A flash of lightning tore through the night, casting her face in a partial silhouette.

"Maybe we should have booked a hotel room after all. I mean —"

Faye interrupted her, "Don't worry Nance. Everything's going to be fine. My co-worker—who's Italian *by the way*—told me all about this place," she offered a smile at her friend's darkening countenance. "And we both know it's cheaper than a hotel.",

"Yeah, but why is no one answering?"

"Don't worry, they will. It's not like there's nobody home. We're at an Abbey, there's *always* someone home."

"I know, Faye. But don't forget, they have only men here. Are you sure they're going to let two sexy hot mamas like us in there?" Nancy replied with a wry smile while puffing up her breasts and shaking her hips.

"Yes. There's the old Nance I remember and love. Good to see your adventurous side coming back," Faye smiled again. "Maybe we can even turn some heads and change some minds."

Nancy laughed but a sudden gust nearly ripped her umbrella from her hand. Though her grip remained firm, the parasol turned inside out and she was bathed by the torrent before finally setting it right.

Faye in the meantime lifted the large brass knocker again and slammed it down in rapid succession. Another jagged bolt pierced the sky and the wind seemed to intensify as thunder rumbled with the sound of an empty dump truck on a bumpy road.

The door opened just as she was in the process of reaching once more for the metal ring, a stern-looking brother dressed in traditional brown robes stared at her. He stepped back to avoid being soaked as another gale blew the pelting rain into the opening. Faye began to enter but stopped when he advanced to block her way.

"Si, che posso fare per te?" he asked, furrowing his brow.

"We're visiting Rome and we were told that you might have some rooms available," she replied and tried to enter again.

From the look on his face, Nancy wasn't sure that he understood, and hoped that with her friend feigning entry he would get the idea. Instead the brother remained rooted to the spot. The only indication he gave that he had heard anything spoken was a slight rise of an eyebrow.

"Do you understand?" Faye asked when he remained motionless.

The monk looked past the two friends into the downpour before shifting his gaze back to give them a quick glance over.

"Mi dispiace, ma non possiamo stanotte. Per favore, torna un altro giorno," he said as he shook his head and started to close the door.

Nancy saw Faye quickly place her foot in the entryway which prevented them from being locked out.

"Look," her friend pleaded. "It's cold and stormy tonight. We don't really want to have to go back to Rome in this darkness. And like I said, we were told that you offered rooms to travelers."

As if to emphasize the urgency, another flash lit up the sky followed closely by the booming rumble of thunder.

Sensing that her friend wouldn't be able to convince him on her own, Nancy added her voice to the issue, "Please," she put in from her position away from the door.

"Mi dispiace, ma non stiamo accettando nessuno. Per favore, torna un'altra volta," the monk replied as he tried to close the door again.

Faye seemed determined not to take no for an answer, and put her knee to the door adding more resistance. "Please, you have to let us in. It's really coming down out here and we were seriously hoping that you would provide a room to us...if only to wait out the storm."

Another flash and peal heightened the point. Nancy watched with hope as her friend began to push on the door with her knee. The monk appeared to resist at first but after a brief and gentle jostling match, he relented and stepped back.

"Un momento, ti passero' qualcuno che parla l'inglese," he said, motioning for them to remain at the dampened entrance.

Turning on his heels, he hurried down the corridor with the echoes from his sandals filling the space of his departure. He rounded a corner to the left and Nancy thought she heard his pace quicken to a run.

The building was quiet save for the occasional crash of lightning and bellow of thunder interspersed between the lashing winds. They removed their wet backpacks and allowed them to slip to the floor before taking in their surroundings. Nancy noticed the vaulted ceiling—that the night and rain had obscured before they were admitted—and stared in wonder at the architecture. The walls were rough-hewn marble, and adorned with a variety of tapestries of saints and other religious paraphernalia. Wooden support beams ran up on either side and into the ceiling. The main hallway itself led approximately forty feet from the entrance to a solid looking door and branched off to the left and right.

"He seemed pretty upset," Faye said. "Maybe we shouldn't be here."

"Hey this was your idea, and you said that your co-worker told you that they let travelers stay."

"Well he told me that they do, but this guy seems a little freaked out. If not for that storm I would've suggested we just left. Maybe stay at a youth hostel or something."

"I don't know about hostels. I still say we should have booked a hotel room before we got here."

"Except that would be more expensive and we both need to count our pennies—I need to count my pennies," Faye corrected.

"What do you think the problem is?" Nancy asked.

"Dunno. Maybe they're not use to two hot chicks showing up in the middle of the night soaking wet and—"

The sound of rapidly approaching footsteps halted her in mid sentence.

"Ho provato a dirlo a loro due, Abate, ci ho provato," the monk returned, trailing behind a stocky fellow with a salt and pepper beard and striking blue eyes.

"Va bene Fratello Fernando, me ne occuperò io," the shorter

man replied, raising his hand and waving the other to silence. He approached the friends and offered a slight bow. "Ladies, I'm Abbot Angelini, how may I be of assistance?" he asked with a thick Italian accent.

"Well," Faye began. "We were told that sometimes you allow travellers to stay here."

"Yes we do under normal circumstances, but as Brother Fernando has told you we are not accepting anyone tonight."

Nancy quickly piped in, "We didn't really understand him. We don't speak Italian."

Though she didn't like lying she reasoned with herself that it wasn't a *complete* lie. She understood a little Italian and had been able to catch only some of what the monk had said.

"I see," Angelini replied. "But tonight is not a good night for allowing guests."

"Please. Look outside," Nancy said.

"I know ladies, but—"

"You can't really expect two girls to travel back to Rome in this type of weather," she interrupted.

The abbot seemed to consider for a few moments, the conflict was evident on his face. Nancy could feel the indecision. She'd been intrigued by Faye's suggestion about staying at an Abbey, but was feeling more and more disappointed the longer Angelini's inner conflict raged. Finally coming to a decision however, the older man folded his lips and turned to Fernando. "Mostrarle in una stanza il più lontano dal nostro lavoro il più possibile."

"Ma Abate, sai cosa stiamo facendo. Il pericolo è noto. Non possono essere autorizzati a rimanere," he replied.

"Lo so Fratello. Ma sono figli di Dio e noi abbiamo la responsabilità di offrire rifugio e assistenza, quando siamo in grado di."

"Sì, Abate, ma non dovremmo davvero—"

Angelini waved Fernando to silence once again. "Dobbiamo Fratello...dobbiamo." The monk bowed to the Abbot and approached the friends. "Brother Fernando will show you to a room. Please stay there for the remainder of the night. In the morning you will be free to explore the monastery but please, I must insist that you both remain in the room until then."

"Thank you," Faye replied. "Thank you very much. We will."

* * *

A lorn wail pierced the night, jolting Nancy awake. She felt somewhat refreshed so guessed that she must have been asleep for some time. Her thoughts were hazy though, like mist in the early morning, and she didn't know if the sound had been in her dreams or not until it was repeated. Fumbling for matches, she lit the lamp then looked to Faye and found her still asleep so she too remained in her bed as the sound came periodically. Something about it however managed to arouse her curiosity, and although she knew that they'd promised to remain in their room, the nagging need to discover what it was finally won out.

Quietly, she got out of bed and began to tiptoe to where her friend lied sleeping. In truth she didn't know why she was being silent, they were in a closed room alone and the cry she'd been hearing was much louder than her bare footsteps. Still, the knowledge that she was about to do something forbidden forced her to continued stealth.

Stumbling over to her bed, she gave her a gentle shake to wake her. At first Faye was unresponsive but after repeated shaking she opened her eyes.

"What?" she asked sleepily.

"Ssh, listen," Nancy whispered.

"What?" her friend repeated.

"Just listen. Listen."

It didn't take long for the cry to come again, and Faye's eyes sprang wide as she bolted upright. "What the hell's that?"

"I don't know, maybe it's their work" Nancy replied. "You wanna go and see?"

"What do you mean by that?" Faye asked.

"I mean, do you want to go and have a look?"

"That's not what I was asking. I meant, what did you mean by *their work*"

Nancy shrugged, "Just that. The Abbot told the brother to give us a room far from their work…or something like that."

"You understood what they'd been saying?"

"Meh…a little," Nancy replied. "Anyway, what do you say? Do you want to go and see?"

"Nancy, we're lucky that they let us stay in the first place. Maybe we shouldn't go snooping around."

"No one's going to see us. Besides, aren't you even curious?"

"That depends. Define curious."

"C'mon you chicken," she teased. "Let's at least see where it's coming from."

"No, we promised that we would stay in our room."

"Look, who's gonna see us? I mean, how many other brothers did we pass on our way here? It looks like the place is deserted."

"That doesn't mean that it is or that we should go asking for trouble."

Nancy feigned innocence, "Who's asking for trouble? And like I said, it's not like anyone is going to see us, and if they do we'll just tell them that we got lost looking for the ladies room."

Seeing that her joke and urging were having the desired effect, she waited and tried to hide her smile.

"Alright, alright. Let me throw something on."

When they were both sufficiently dressed, Nancy doused the lamp and gingerly eased the door opened to peek out.

"Let's go, the coast is clear."

Together they inched from their room and waited for the sound to come again. When it did, they proceeded down the hall in its direction. The candelabra placed in wall sockets at intervals elongated their shadows as they passed.

They rounded a curve in the hall and came to a juncture leading to the right and left. There they waited again for the sound to return. When it did, they gauged the direction and continued their stealthy progress in search of its source.

Nancy's heart was pounding from the thrill of sneaking around the seemingly deserted monastery. Her mind was occupied with the thought of locating what was making the noise, though she couldn't understand why it was so important to her. It was like the lure of a Siren song calling her to a reward, so on she crept with her accomplice in tow.

After some time, they approached a right turn as the wail arose once more. This time it was accompanied by voices. Nancy risked a peek around the corner in time to see the Abbot and Brother Fernando emerge from a room and close the door behind them.

She did her best to steady her breathing as the excitement of the moment nearly got the better of her. The desire to rush headlong into the hall was nearly uncontrollable, like a treasure hunter clearing the final obstacle and locating the legendary King Solomon's mines. She somehow forced herself to remain calm and continued to watch.

The Abbot turned to the monk and placed a hand upon his shoulder, "Fratello Fernando, è finito. Entro domani se ne andrà per sempre."

"Sì Abate. E pagherei volentieri il prezzo cento volte," the brother replied.

Together they began to grope their way along the wall towards where the two trespassers waited.

She immediately noticed the change. The Abbot's eyes, which had once been a piercing blue, were now a milky white, as were those of the monk's.

Nancy almost stumbled over Faye—who had also poked her head around the corner—as she quickly tried to retreat and back into a recess in the wall.

The two women sunk themselves in as far as the space would allow and waited for the men to pass. They held their breaths when four fingers appeared at one edge of their hiding place and Brother Fernando shambled into view, his hand waved in the open air as he sought the other side of the alcove.

The Abbot came next, and like the member of his flock, he too waved a hand in the opening, but unlike Fernando, he paused and turned his blind eyes upon the two spies. Nancy's heart was beating so loudly that she thought the newly-blinded man would hear it. He remained for a few seconds longer, staring expressionlessly at them, before feeling his way past and on around the corner.

As soon as they were out of sight the howl came again from the recently vacated room. Nancy looked after them then stepped out of the inlet to continue her search. She was so close to finding the answer to the burning yet unknown desire. It was something that was more than simple curiosity. It was like destiny, something she was fated to do. Behind her, she felt Faye's grip on her shoulder and momentarily halted.

"What are you doing?" her friend asked, "That was too close. We shouldn't be here!"

"We came all this way Faye. We might as well find out what's causing all that ruckus."

"But did you see their eyes? And what were they saying?" Faye continued

"Yes I did."

"And that doesn't bother you?"

"No, in fact it makes me even more curious."

"I don't believe you Nance! C'mon, let's get out of here," Faye pleaded.

"Oh stop being a chicken. We'll just take a peek inside the room and leave."

"And what were they saying? You never answered."

"I don't know. Something about something being gone tomorrow and being willing to pay the price a thousand times...or something like that."

Nancy pulled away and continued towards the door. She stopped with her hand on the knob and motioned for Faye to catch up. With her friend and co-conspirator at her side, she started to open the door as the wail came again. Faye stiffened behind her, but undaunted and overcome with curiosity, she turned the handle and started to poke her head around the door.

There was another howl and a sudden rush of wind that knocked her into her friend and both landed in a tangled heap against the opposite wall.

* * *

The sound of agitated voices speaking Italian wafted through the darkness as Nancy began to regain consciousness. She opened her eyes to find Faye and herself surrounded by a host of robed figures, including the recently blinded monk and Abbot.

The brother was frantic, "They've released it Abbot, they've released it!"

"Maybe, maybe not," Angelini replied. "Quickly, check to see if the article is still there"

"What can we do Abbot?"

"Check for the article, and pray, Brother Fernando."

The monk ran his hands through his hair then felt his way into the room.

After a short time he returned a little calmer than he'd entered, "Yes, it's still there. But he's gone."

Concern stitched across Angelini's face like an approaching tempest, and he momentarily closed his sightless eyes. "That is both fortunate and unfortunate. However, he could not have gotten far in his condition. We will send someone to find him."

"What about these two?" Fernando asked, his recently gained calm evaporating. "What if it follows one of them?"

"I do not think it will. They were unconscious so I believe they will be safe. The storm is over, have Brother Madara take them to the city."

The monk would not relent, "Are you sure Abbot? Are you sure that they will be safe...that their malicious interference hasn't brought doom down upon us all?"

Nancy slowly climbed to her feet then extended a hand to help Faye stand as well. At a gesture from Angelini, four brothers gently but firmly brought the ladies to stand before him as though in judgement.

The older man's voice was stern when he changed to speak to them in English, "Why did you leave your room last night? You were given express instructions to remain there until the morning. Why did you disobey?"

Filled with a mixture of uneasiness, fear and shame, Nancy Carmen looked at her friend before replying, "Well...we...we heard something."

"What did you hear?"

"We heard what sounded like someone in trouble or in pain. We just wanted to see if there was something we could do to help because we'd noticed that there weren't many people here last night."

The Abbot shook his head, "You should not have left your room. You should have remained as instructed."

"Yes, I—" Faye started to interject, but Nancy didn't give her a chance to finish.

"Yes, I know. And we're sorry, but we were only trying to help," she said as she cast a sharp look at her friend.

Angelini was unwavering, "What happened when you opened that door?" he indicated the room behind where he stood, "Did you see anything? Did you feel anything?"

Though she was a little confused and her mind was slightly groggy, his words triggered a slow recollection of the two of them attempting to open the door. She remembered the gust of wind and being knocked across the hall. Nancy remained silent for a few moments longer, and when she could think more clearly she responded, "No. We didn't see anything, and the only thing we felt was wind knocking us out,"

"And now?" Angelini asked.

She looked at Faye for confirmation before answering. The

questions were strange and she was beginning to curse the still unknown curiosity that had driven her the previous night. Seeing her friend's blank stare didn't do much as far as putting her mind at ease, but at least she felt confident that they were together in their feelings.

"Um...nothing," she said at last.

It was now the Abbot's turn to be silent and Nancy was worried that he might enter into another flurry of questions, like an overzealous prosecutor. His eyes searched them both as though he could discern the truth from their outward appearance even though he was sightless.

When he finally spoke, his voice had returned to the calm manner that had greeted them the night before, "Very well. But you will have to leave this place now. We cannot abide with you disobeying our rules. Brother Madara!"

A tall monk stepped forward and the conversation momentarily returned to their native Italian. "Yes, Abbot."

"These ladies will be leaving now. Please see them safely to the city," he then turned his attention back to Faye and Nancy, "Goodbye ladies, and may God's blessings be upon you. I hope that you will enjoy the remainder of your time here in Italy."

Faye was the first to answer, "Thank you…and…" she looked at Nancy before continuing. "Sorry that we disobeyed you. Um… are you okay? I mean…your eyes...what happened to you—both of you?"

Angelini shook his head and smiled, "Alas ladies, what has happened to us is nothing to concern yourselves with. Brother Madara will escort you safely to the city. Be well ladies."

* * *

Almost three weeks later the friends were boarding a plane for home with the events of that night all but forgotten. Nancy had to admit that despite the rocky start to their tour of Italy, the remainder of their stay had been very enjoyable. This was one place that she could now remove from her list of destinations to visit before death came to call. They took their seats and shortly afterwards were taxiing down the runway for takeoff. It was then, that out of the corner of her eye, she saw it.

CHAPTER 3

The dirt that hung in the air was tainted red and created an unnatural dusk. Several mountain ridges lined the distance and many of them were erupting. Magma and flaming boulders spewed from their craters and streaked back towards the ground. Overhead, the sky was clouded and undulating as though a giant held it by its edges and fanned it like a bedsheet.

Everywhere Peter Gentrick turned he was greeted by the same destruction. It was akin to standing in the aftermath of a forest fire as wisps of smoke curled from the scorched soil around and below him. The invasive odour of sulphur and burned wood made it difficult for him to breathe.

Instinct told him that he couldn't remain where he was, that he had to move, so he started to make his way down the hill and into the ruined countryside. The further down he walked, the more he realized that the ground below was not flat, but lined with craggy mounds and held a smaller hill. Anything that might have grown was now long dead; more than likely consumed by the same flames or volcanic eruptions that had ravaged the landscape.

It was strange to be in such a place, and stranger still to hold no fear of it. Even when another flaming boulder crashed to the ground in the near distance, sending up a burst of dirt and debris, he remained calm, as somehow he knew he'd be safe. When he reached the bottom, Peter turned to look back, and for a moment thought he saw a pair of eyes staring at him through the billowing clouds.

A high-pitched squeal drew his attention and he turned in time to see what at first looked like a possum, but the gaping toothy mouth that lined its back told him he was wrong. The thing was scurrying towards his booted foot with its maw snapping open and close. Reflexively he kicked it away and it landed on its back—or mouth as the case may be—close to a waist-high ridge. Before it could right itself, a pale hand reached over and seized it. Then a bowling ball shaped head with two round black eyes in its centre and three smaller ones on either side popped up. The eyes looked at him, blinking in harmless innocence while the possum-like creature squealed in protest.

The thing holding it—perhaps sensing that Peter was not a threat, or at least not going to try to claim its prize—fully emerged from its hiding place. It had six human arms, three on each side of its torso, which gave it the appearance of a crab but without the pincers. Its round head was attached to its body by a thin neck, and it perched on the ridge with its five free hands clasping the sharp, blackened rock.

The top half of its head flipped open like the lid of a treasure chest, and it plunged the possum creature inside. It then reclosed and devoured the thing with an audible crunching of bones as it continued to regard him with that same innocence.

Suddenly it charged, shrieking as it came, and revealing two rows of triangular shaped teeth. The creature scuttled sideways, moving dextrously over pits and lumps.

Peter dodged aside, and to his horror heard similar cries echoed from the direction the thing had come. He didn't wait to see how many had responded, instead he pelted down the hill and tried to be careful not to trip or twist his ankle on the many obstacles that sat in his way.

Some smaller rocks, apparently kicked loose by his pursuers tumbled past him, making him take a quick glance over his shoulder. His heart shuddered when he saw that he was being chased by an uncountable number of the things. They were scuttling, screeching, and creating chaos in their wake.

The terrain began to level, allowing him to run faster with less fear of injury, though there were numerous charred husks of trees that he'd have to negotiate his way around. As he closed on the first of the burned ruins, he saw another of the possum creatures crawl from a hole near the top. The thing sprang at him, but he was able to knock it aside. Moments later he heard its death cry and knew that one of the crab-creatures had made a meal of it.

An unexpected dip in the ground caused him to stumble and fall, but he used the momentum to roll back onto his feet. His knees were bruised but he did his best to ignore the pain as each step stung like hot needles shooting through his kneecaps.

From the corner of his eye he saw three of the man-crabs scuttling towards him on the right. Fear gripped him like a vice and he changed direction in an attempt to put as much distance as possible between his pursuers and himself. He wished that more of the possum creatures were available to act as distraction, but he was not to be so lucky.

Once he cleared the burned forest, he came to a pitted and furrowed field with what looked like a partially walled courtyard on the opposite side. The structure was damaged in places at the top and there were gaping holes in its sides. From his position, Peter could see no sign of the house the yard may have belonged to.

The ground leading to it reminded him of rice paddies he'd seen on TV, and he knew once again that he would have to use care while crossing. Close behind, he could hear the things chasing him as their hand-like feet made slapping sounds on the charred earth, and their shrieking sent icicles racing up and down his spine. Peter didn't know what he would find in the seemingly abandoned courtyard, but he prayed there would be some type of weapon inside as well as none of the creatures.

He was nearly across the field when one of his pursuers scuttled in front of him from the left and tried to bar his way. Instinctively, he planted his right foot firmly on the ground then sprang to his left. The manoeuvre was successful and he was able to get around the crab-thing. The volume of their screeching was nearly ear shattering and almost threw him off his stride, but he found his balance and hurtled towards the wall.

When he was close enough to a broken section, Peter threw himself through the opening, but unfortunately he'd misjudged the height of the bottom of the hole and caught his left foot. Once again he tucked and rolled into a ball and came to rest on his knees. Pain flooded through him and he closed his eyes, covered his head with his hands and waited for the man-crabs to begin mauling him. To his surprise nothing happened.

Heart pounding and sweat covering his body, Gentrick slowly removed his head from its shelter and looked around. Outside of the courtyard, a multitude of man-crabs were scurrying like ants, but none dared to cross the threshold of the enclosure. It was at least one thing to be thankful for—as puzzling as it was. He tried not to think of what could deter such creatures from continuing their chase. There were more pressing concerns, chief among which was how he was going to eventually escape from them because he knew he'd not be able to stay where he was forever.

Seeing that he was safe for the moment, Peter decided to explore in the hopes of finding that desperately needed weapon. His cursory survey of the yard didn't lift his spirits very high however. Directly opposite of where he'd entered was a boulder nearly twice as tall as he was, and a girth of enormous proportions. If it had come from an eruption it was a wonder that anything was still standing.

A well sat nearly in the centre of the yard. Its stones were scorched like everything he'd seen so far, but it looked sturdy and made him wonder if there might still be some water inside. It was of course a little farfetched to imagine a sword or better yet, an AR-15 with plenty of ammunition concealed at its bottom. Some shoots of scraggy plants that somehow survived what so much else hadn't, were close to its base.

As he started walking he realized that the yard was actually larger than he'd first thought. Since he was never very good at estimating measurements he didn't wager a guess at its dimensions. Three sets of stairs on different sides of the enclosure led to a platform that ran along all four walls. Granted it was broken in places here and there, and the damage seemed as much from age as from stones spewed from the volcanic activity, but perhaps it would be strong enough to hold his weight and allow him a better view of the countryside. Not that he expected to see anything that he'd not seen from the top of the hill, but it would at least give him a view of just how screwed he was.

Peter approached the closest staircase which happened to be on the same side he'd entered, and started to climb. He realized quickly however that several of the steps close to the top were missing, making it impossible for him to reach the platform. Cursing his bad luck, he retreated and surveyed the other two before he approached either.

Seeing that the flight directly across from where he stood and to the left of the boulder seemed to have the least damage, he decided to take his chances. As he crossed the yard he saw that the number of creatures outside of his sanctuary had multiplied, and in true crab fashion were climbing on top of each other. Their constant screeching was unnerving but he did his best to remain calm even though from time to time his legs would buckle as a thread of fear would race through him.

He reached the stairs and began to climb again. It was strange to see that despite some type of inferno having gutted the area, the wood on the stairs somehow managed to avoid being completely consumed. In fact, it seemed to have suffered only mild damage, as though something had shielded it from the worst of the flames. A single step near the top was broken, but bracing his right arm against the wall, Peter was able to safely reach the riser above it and emerge onto the platform.

As expected, there was nothing to see except rolling flame-damaged hills and more of the scuttling man-crabs closing in. His heart sank at the sight and he fought to keep his bladder from releasing. He continued to look around in dismay when something in the distance caught his attention. At first he thought it was his eyes playing tricks on him, but when he concentrated, he became sure that they weren't. On the far horizon, past the belching volcanoes, Peter Gentrick saw the green of a forest or a pasture between two mountain peaks. It was in stark contrast to the muted red of the atmosphere and burned landscape, but it was there and it offered a ray of hope. The only problem was how he was going to evade the horde that had him surrounded.

Despair settled upon him like a musty cloak, making it difficult to breathe and his chest to constrict. His situation was dire, but if he gave in to it, he truly would be lost. He had to find some way out of his predicament, though he wasn't quite sure where he was or how he'd gotten there. There seemed to be a hole in his memory. He couldn't remember anything before he'd opened his eyes to his ruined surroundings. The only thing he was sure of was himself. He knew that he was a man...a man named Peter...Peter Gentrick. Everything else was as empty as a freshly washed whiteboard.

The man-crabs below were scampering back and forth, looking up at him but clearly afraid of both touching the walls of the courtyard and crossing its threshold. Their mouths continued to open unnaturally wide and their shrill cries echoed all around. When Peter walked along the platform, the horde kept pace with him, yammering, scuttling, and crawling over each other.

He turned back toward the mammoth boulder and once again thought he was being deceived, though this time by the play of the ruddy light and shadows. It had to be a trick, he told himself, but the more he looked, the clearer it became. Then reality took hold and he reasoned that although what he was seeing might be real, it was not a guarantee that it would be of any use. Still, he had nothing to lose so he returned to the ground and approached the stone. Again, he wondered how it had gotten there and started to think that perhaps it was not accidental after all.

Walking around to the right of the block, he found not only that there were indeed stairs, but also that there was enough room for him to pass. On his way down the steps, he paused and wished he'd a torch or something to light his way. He also wished again for a weapon, should there be anything lurking below. Though his mind began to cloud with fear, he realized that he would be just as dead if he remained where he was, so Peter forced himself back into motion.

The stairs went further than he'd thought, and when he reached the bottom, he found that the dull rays from above were able to dimly light the area. Beneath the yard the air was cool but stale, and his feet kicked up dust that had lain undisturbed for perhaps millennia.

It swirled around him and threatened to choke him even as he waved his hands to fan it away. Removing his shirt, he wrapped it around his mouth and nose before taking another step. The aroma of his body odour wasn't much better than the unfiltered air, but at least he wouldn't suffocate from the dust.

He took a few hesitant steps away from the stairs to examine the right wall of the passage. It was knotted and pitted at regular very close intervals as though its constructor had taken a trowel and scooped out stone two to three fingers' distance apart. Peter looked to the opposite wall and found the same manor of construction. When his eyes moved to the top he stared in apprehension. The tunnel was not constructed of stone, but of human bones laid horizontally one on top of the other. Between the top of the wall and the ceiling were skulls placed side by side but with their lower jaws missing.

His first impulse was to run out of the tunnel and back into the courtyard, but he quickly came to the conclusion that it was the despair of being trapped by the man-crabs that had brought him down below in the first place. Digging deep for his resolve, he remained.

The way ahead was dark and more than likely wouldn't go very far in any case, so he began to cautiously walk. Once he'd moved some distance from the stairs, the tunnel turned black as pitch and fear of stumbling or worse, forced him to cling to the bone wall for security. He also did his best not to let his imagination wander and create hidden monsters waiting for him to fall into their grasps.

Peter had been walking sightless in the darkness when the sudden sound of footsteps behind him shattered his confidence and caused his heart to leap from his chest. With his breath held lest the sound give away his location to whatever was stalking him, he waited and prayed. Part of him hoped the sound would come again so that he would know how far away they were, while at the same time dreaded its return.

When he could hold it no longer, he release his breath as slowly and quietly as he could and nearly jumped again when he heard its slight echo. Every inhalation and exhalation sounded louder than the one before, even the accelerated beating of his heart seemed to crash from the walls.

As the footsteps didn't return, he began to slowly move again but froze once more when he heard them anew. As before, the follower stopped with him and seemed to wait while he waited. The pounding of his heart grew so loud in his own ears that he imagined his head would explode. His slow breathing echoed around him like a noisy companion and he turned around as quietly as he could.

Through the dim light from the distant staircase he saw that the passageway was empty, and realized the sound of footsteps he'd heard were his own bouncing from the skeletal walls.

Cursing his stupidity he resumed groping his way along the tunnel. He didn't know how far he'd traveled when a faint glow appeared ahead. At first he thought it another hallucination, like the footsteps that had been following him. Additionally, it wasn't the same ruby hue that he'd been bathed in earlier. This was light, regular light, the type that could be seen on an ordinary day and, it seemed to be spilling —albeit palely—from what looked like a tunnel on the left.

Peter resisted the urge to quicken his pace, and kept his hand feeling along the bones until he was close enough to be sure that there truly was a connecting passageway. Changing sides, he refused to think of the material he'd been running his hand along and instead focused on the brighter aspect that perhaps there was an exit and safety close by. There was also the possibility of other horrors prowling just around the corner, but he refused to consider such things as well.

When he was close enough, rather than rushing inside, he

used caution and slowly stuck his head around the wall. He was relieved that he didn't see anything other than another macabre tunnel —though considerably shorter than the one he was in. The sudden thoughts of who could have built such things, why, and how many bodies had been used entered his mind and he wondered why it hadn't occurred to him earlier. At the same time he tried not to consider that people may have been killed in order to supply building material, but couldn't keep his mind from straying in that direction.

Pulling himself back to the moment, Peter saw that the short passageway opened into a larger room. Casting a last look back the way he'd come, he stepped softly into the new tunnel and continued to grope along the wall. When he noticed that there was sufficient light to see, he quickly dropped his hand from the bones and instinctively wiped both on his pants.

The next place he found himself in was a circular room constructed of the same material. Dominating this space were five pillars of enormous circumference and spanning from floor to ceiling. Naturally, they too were made of bones and skulls, and on the floor surrounding each of them were individual pools of water. Closer inspection showed that the pillars and walls were not circular but were in fact flat surfaced.

He walked around the colonnades and counted five sides on each. Four of the structures seemed to be plain-faced, containing only knobby bones and skulls, but the fifth held something that he couldn't readily identify. It may have been the mummified remains of a dog or some other four-legged animal fastened to the balustrade. The thing had a long protruding muzzle and spikes lining its back. One of its front hands or paws was visible and it contained razor-sharp claws. Its tail, which was frozen into an 'S' shape, ended in hooks. Although the thing didn't appear to be very large, Gentrick was certain that had it been alive it would easily have made short work of him.

The water around this pillar was the source of the light. Peter looked into it and tried to gauge its depth or perhaps find what was illuminating it, but the brightness made it difficult to determine either. It also was not wide, and had there been a landing at the base of the column, he could have easily jumped onto it—had it contained a door, that is. Unfortunately, there was nothing that he could see that would offer such salvation and he highly doubted that he would find it at the bottom of the water.

Staring into the shimmering liquid, he felt dryness at the back of his throat and, for a moment considered the implications of drinking from this strange source. The water though was obviously not stagnant because its slight ripple indicated that there was a current moving somewhere beneath.

Despite that logic he was nonetheless hesitant, but the burning thirst forced him to turn caution aside, so he knelt and dipped one hand into the pool. It was surprisingly cold and sent a shock coursing through him as a snippet of a vision danced at the outskirts of his memory. He tried to grasp it and draw it in like a fish nibbling on a hook but all that came to him were a pair of green eyes.

Peter removed his shirt from his face, cupped his hands, and drank. The next thing he knew, his mind was reeling from dizziness as though he'd spun in circles. He climbed to his feet to try to walk off the vertigo but succeeded only in falling to his hands and knees. His second attempt was more successful, though he swayed and stumbled his way around the room.

Fearing that he would crash to the floor without support, he moved to the nearest wall and leaned against it while he tried to centre himself. As his giddiness ebbed he became aware that he'd been breathing rapidly, nearly hyperventilating, so he took slower, deeper breaths.

A sudden movement out of the corner of his eye cause his heart to nearly freeze. Peter turned and saw the mummified creature walking down from its place on the pillar, the empty sockets where its eyes had been were intent upon him. Additional movement in the room made the blood rush to his head and his delirium to increase. Similar creatures stalked down towards the waters from the other pillars. That he could see the knobby bones of the column's construction through their bodies made them more frightening.

The first beast was now on the floor and bounding towards him. When it was within a few metres it sprang with its tail whipping the air and its arms and legs raking at the empty space between it and its prey. He tried to avoid the attack but his unsteadiness made his movements sluggish. One of the creature's talons ripped into his left shoulder blade, knocking him painfully to the ground. When Peter tried to crawl away the other things closed on him and barred his escape.

A claw bit into his ankle and twisted him onto his back. He looked up into the face of the mummified thing, and to his continued horror it had grown and now towered over him.

A voice like a straw bristled broom on cement pounded in his ears, "The end of man draws near. The initiate has been chosen...the convocation has begun!"

The bleating of his alarm tore Peter from his nightmare. Beside him his wife Catherine had already begun to stir. The dream and the words spoken still hung in his mind, as vivid as a cinema screen.

"The end of man draws near. The initiate has been chosen...the convocation has begun!"

It was chilling and something that he wouldn't soon forget.

"Another nightmare?" Catherine asked.

"Yeah," he sighed, the look on his face must have been obvious.

"Maybe it's your conscience eating at you."

Oh God, this again, he thought to himself as he watched her climb from their bed and leave the room. *Why can't she just try to understand?* As the words entered his mind he knew the futility of the notion.

Catherine Gentrick was like a pit bull when she locked onto an idea, and since the night he'd come home and couldn't tell her where he'd been, she'd convinced herself that he was lying to her. The truth was that he simply couldn't remember. He recalled watching the hockey game at a bar but couldn't remember which bar. In fact he couldn't even remember driving to it, walking in, ordering drinks, sitting down...anything. It was as though someone had taken a laser and precisely eradicated those few hours from his life.

His lack of recollection was nearly as maddening as his wife's persistence that he'd not gone, that he was hiding something from her. Indeed it had been a difficult week, and he could see no end in sight as long as that night continued to elude him. Truth be told, even if he finally did remember, deep down he knew that she still wouldn't believe him. Peter found himself sometimes wondering how they had even managed to stay married for so long. The only thing he really had to be thankful for was that she continued to cook and clean for him, but at the moment even that didn't make him feel any better.

Looking back on the past week, it was disappointing how his life had changed, and most importantly his sleep. His dreams have been the same from almost the time of that missing night. He would find himself in a strange land, a ruined land that he somehow felt was the world—the earth. Different horrors would chase him and he'd run for his life and nearly piss himself. It's a wonder that he even managed to hold his bladder in the real world.

He felt it had something to do with those lost memories and briefly considered going to a psychiatrist to be hypnotised. Unfortunately he held little faith in that particular aspect of the practice. Whenever he'd heard about people undergoing hypnosis he'd always scoffed at it as being fake and both the practitioners and the subjects as fraudsters.

No, he'd figure it out for himself. Something that he will see or hear will jog his memory and lift the fog from his mind.

As much as he dreaded the day ahead, he pulled himself out of bed and prepared for work. While he dressed, he found that he couldn't decide if he wanted a busy day at the shop or a slow one. Being busy would keep his mind occupied, but it would also make his return to sleep and dreams seem that much quicker. A slow one however, would allow him to think and hopefully remember. That alternative also had its drawbacks because he was confident that it would lead to more frustration at what he was sure would be his failure to recall the missing night.

With a shake of his head he buttoned his shirt and went to the bathroom to wash his face and brush his teeth. When he was finished, he made his way to the kitchen, and was happy to see Catherine making his breakfast—at least he thought it was for him. After he sat down, she prepared coffee and placed it on the table. He wished that the doubt wasn't so clearly written on her face because it would have made the meal more enjoyable.

As he sipped at the steaming liquid through the aftertaste of toothpaste, his wife scooped the eggs she'd been frying from the pan, and took the two slices of bread from the toaster as it popped. Placing them onto the same plate, she none too gently put the dish in front of him. Peter's consolation was that she'd not slammed it down the way she had on previous days. Perhaps things would be cooling down soon.

He began to eat and she placed herself in the chair across from him with a cup of her own. When he looked up he saw that her face had changed to a semblance of worry and he didn't know what to expect next.

"Just tell me if it's over," she sighed.

"What? What are you talking about?" he couldn't keep the surprise from his voice.

His wife gave a sad smile as she repeated, "Just tell me if it's over."

"If what's over? What are you talking about?"

She sighed again. "Us, Peter...us...if we're over...if our marriage is through."

"Oh God, Catherine, I love you," he dropped the partially eaten toast onto his plate and scrubbed his face with his hand. The fact that crumbs scratched at his skin didn't bother him. "Why would you think that it's over?"

"C'mon, Peter, there's only one reason why you *can't remember* that night and we both know it, so I just want you to tell me if it's over. I don't want to be made a fool of anymore than I already have been."

"Oh, please stop this, Catherine. Why would you even think such a thing? Why can't you—no—why *won't* you try to understand what I'm going through?"

She slammed her hand onto the table causing the dish to jump and his coffee to nearly spill, "Because, Peter, it's strange that you say you can't remember! You could've come up with a better lie than that, couldn't you?"

"That's exactly the point...that's exactly the point! I *could* have come up with a better lie, if I were lying. So the fact that I told you that I can't remember, then maybe...just *maybe*...I'm not lying."

She remained silent and he searched her face for some sign that he might finally be getting through. He knew her personality well. They'd been together for fifteen years but married for only seven. In that time he'd seen the best and worst of her. When she wasn't doubting him, their relationship was good…great in fact.

Peter had known that Catherine was the one for him from their first date. There had been a kind of childish innocence to her that had told him that she would love him for who he was rather than what he had. He knew the value of such love because it had been something he'd wanted and missed nearly all of his life. Material things were meaningless to her as she was very content to be the wife of an auto mechanic. Some of her other boyfriends—she'd told him—had been on their way to successful careers, either in business or finance, but she'd said a life that they could have offered was not something that she'd ever wanted.

"Look," he said, after enduring her continued silence. "I have to figure out what happened to me, and I'm sorry, but you're really not helping any." Peter pushed away from the table and stood, "I'm going to work now, maybe on the way it'll come back to me. But I know there's something wrong with me. I just know it. And until I can figure it out, there's nothing more I can add except to tell you that I simply don't know what happened that night. And what I really need now is your support to help me figure it out."

There was a slight softening to her expression, and though he wasn't flooded with relief, he was able to acknowledge to himself that at least it was a start.

* * *

As he piloted his car down the busy street, he played that fateful day back in his mind. It had begun like every other in his life. He'd awoken, eaten, gone to work, gone home. Wait. Something nibbled on the edge of his memory. Plans. That's it. He'd plans to watch the game...but with whom?

It was the closest he'd come so far to remembering, so he tried to keep that thread of recall going. It was like when he'd been in elementary school and had fallen into the deep end of the pool, he'd barely been able to swim and had panicked. He'd kicked and kicked and tried to surface enough to grab hold of the edge of the deck and haul himself to safety. His first few attempts had been unsuccessful, and he'd thought that he would drown, but he'd kept trying until first one hand then the other had closed firmly on the edge of the pool and he'd saved himself. If he kept kicking at the hole in his memory, then maybe he'd be able to grasp those missing hours and put them back where they belonged.

Peter was so lost in his efforts that he had to jam both feet onto the brake to avoid rear-ending the car in front of him. As much as he hated to let go of the thread that he'd finally been able to wrap a fragment of his mind around, he decided to focus on driving and save everything else for later. The decision turned out to be a good one because shortly after traffic began to move again, he narrowly avoided colliding with another driver who'd changed lanes seemingly without looking. He was going to honk and swear at the man, but instead chose to concede that karma had evened out the near-mishaps.

* * *

As expected, it was an enormous effort to concentrate on his work at the garage. There were several instances when he found himself having to redo something that he'd been accustomed to doing, and in fact had done perfectly well many times before. His coworkers and even his boss mentioned to him that he seemed distracted.

When the day ended he was more relieved than usual, but at the same time a small part of him wasn't looking forward to his evening with Catherine. He hoped that she would be more reasonable, though he knew better than to expect it.

His mind drifted to the dreams that have been plaguing him, and once again he felt that they were somehow connected to his lost night. How, was a question he couldn't readily answer, but the more he thought about it, the more sense it started to make.

He forced himself from such notions as he wound his way through rush hour traffic, but he did make a plan. Maybe if he could piece together the sequence of his nightmares there may be a clue hidden within them.

Peter suddenly recalled a friend from college who'd been a follower of dream interpretation. It'd been a number of years since they'd last spoken but he was sure that she would be able to help him, or at the very least point him in the direction of someone who could. He was certain that he would be able to find a way of contacting her, and with luck she would still be open to talking with him. It's not that they had parted on bad terms or that there had ever been anything other than friendship between them. *Still,* he told himself, *people are different and you could never be sure how they'll react to being rung up out of the blue.*

Setting aside that thought as well, he focused more on the road and reaching his house safely.

When he arrived home, there was the expected hostility

from his wife, but at least dinner had been made. The conversation while they ate was stilted, and when he couldn't stand it any longer, he risked outlining his plan.

"So, is she who you went to see?" Catherine spat.

"Oh for fuck's sake, would you stop it!" the combined stress was beginning to take its toll.

Instead of replying, she rose from the table and stamped into the bedroom, slamming the door behind her. He thought about going after her, but decided against it because it would only lead to more fighting, and he had better things to do before he entered that desolate landscape of his dreams. And he had little doubt that he wouldn't.

After finishing dinner alone and clearing the table, he got a pen and pad from a kitchen drawer and began writing down as much of the things from his nightmares as he could. He started with the ruined land, the undulating sky with its red dusky atmosphere, the bone-tomb, man-crabs and most importantly the strange creatures from the columns. As he recalled them, something surged through him and he couldn't get rid of the feeling again that they were somehow the key to the mysterious hole in his memory.

Abruptly he stood, shook himself and began to pace the room. What was he thinking? What was happening to him? This wasn't some sort of supernatural situation. There wasn't anyone trying to communicate with him through his dreams. He really needed to get a grip on himself before he lost his mind completely. His problem was temporary memory loss, nothing more. Those creatures from his dreams were not anything real, they were merely a representation of something that he didn't or couldn't put his finger on. Hopefully his college friend, Alison would be able to help shed some light on everything.

When he was sure that he could continue without his over-active imagination getting the better of him, Peter sat back down and resumed bringing the details of his dream to the surface. He was surprised by just how much he actually remembered.

They all began with him on a hill in a burned land. He was always chased to the same abandoned courtyard and would make his way into the boned catacombs. The first time though, he'd not found the pillars because a noise like a grated scream, had forced him awake. The second time, he'd found the pillars, but the ethereal creatures jumping from them had woken him. Last night one of them had been real—at least real in his dream—and as much as he hated to admit to the thought, it really did seem as if someone or something *were* trying to communicate with him. Show him a progression of things, and judging by the way they'd chosen, it was more than likely something that would not be pleasant.

Gentrick found himself suddenly not wanting to go to sleep anymore for fear of what would happen next, where he'd be taken and what horrors he'd be forced to see before waking.

He needed answers, but could he do it? Could he actually call Alison with Catherine thinking the way she was? Plus, why was he so sure that he'd be able to find her number. He'd lost it long ago, and though other friends might have it, did he really want to go that route? If one of them were to tell his wife that he'd called looking for another woman's number, he was sure that she would take it as more humiliation—which in some ways was understandable. What would she do then?

No, maybe he could find answers some other way. If he couldn't, then he would have to try to find her number and run the risk of Catherine's wrath.

Changing his line of thought, Peter walked to the living room and opened his laptop. While the device booted, he said a silent curse for not having purchased a faster one. However, he'd never been much of a consumer and only chose to buy things as he needed them instead of as soon as the newest models came out.

His mind began to drift again but his computer's login screen saved it from straying too far. He had to key in his password twice because his agitated state caused him to enter it incorrectly the first time. Several seconds later he was able to access the internet. His first searches weren't very successful, but after he calmed himself and focused, he was able to get better results. They were still not what he needed so he narrowed it down, and was more successful as a litany of information flashed onto the page.

Peter's logical mind instantly began to assert itself, equating people in such profession as being not much different from palm readers, fortune tellers and all out charlatans. With effort, he managed to quash such thoughts but didn't dismiss them entirely. He was not about to be taken for a fool or an easy mark.

Sometime ago he'd learned the value of reviews and recommendations. Granted it had been after he'd in fact been taken by con artists on two occasions but they were lessons well learned. After reading some reviews and—as expected—finding that the owners of the businesses were indeed dishonest, he finally found one that had *some* credibility. A quick phone call saw him able to make an appointment for that evening.

Catherine came out of the room as he was preparing to leave, "Was that *her* on the phone?"

"No, it wasn't."

"Then where are you going?"

"I'm going to see a different dream interpreter."

"Sure you are!"

Her venom hadn't eased.

"If you don't believe me, then you're welcome to come with me."

"No thanks. I don't want to see you and your lover."

"Oh shut the fuck up!"

It was the first time he'd ever spoken to his wife in such a way. They'd had their share of arguments over the years, same as any other couple, but never had he spoken so abusively to her.

The surprised look on her face was quickly replaced with fury, "How dare you sp—"

Peter didn't give her a chance to finish, "Look, I'm fucking sick of this," his anger was almost uncontrollable, "You're fuckin' doubting me, doubting what I'm telling, and when I give you the chance to see for yourself so we can end this shit, this is how you react!"

Catherine tried to speak again, but her husband rode over her, "I'm sick of this!" he roared, "There's something fuckin' wrong with me, I'm missing a night of my life and instead of being concerned or even supportive, you're acting like a fuckin' jealous child. Now get your fuckin' shoes on because you're coming with me so that you can see for yourself that I've been telling you the truth all along."

She continued to stare shocked silence at him, but when he started to speak again, she quickly went to gather her shoes and purse. He told himself that hated speaking to her like that—though a part of him took some pleasure in releasing the stress that had been building.

Peter finished putting his own shoes on and was going to check the address again on his Smartphone, but the thought of her coming in just as he was either doing it, or putting it away was enough to change his mind. Instead he decided to wait until she asked where there were going before he would check the address and directions.

As expected, when she'd purse in hand and shoes on her feet, Catherine none too gently asked where they were going. Instead of answering immediately, he waited until they were driving, then handed her his phone and asked her to open the webpage and give him directions. He was fairly certain that he knew where it was, but with her helping him, hopefully it would dispel whatever lingering doubts she might have.

Although the look of scepticism remained on her face, she nonetheless complied. Peter sighed inwardly at the thought that he might be finally getting through to her.

The dream interpreter was located in a nondescript bungalow on a semi-busy street. It occurred to him that he'd passed it many times but it had always been part of the background. Now it was like a lighthouse shining through fog as he stared at a pink neon rendition of a crystal ball sitting on a blue stand. The image dominated the centre of the large solitary window, while a small placard in a lower corner indicated tarot reading and dream interpretation.

When he looked at his wife, the expression on her face had changed to something unreadable.

"Maybe you should see a psychiatrist, I'm sure that it would be better than...*this*."

"I don't need a shrink. They don't believe in anything other than childhood trauma as being the reason why we go to see them."

"Well maybe—"

"No," he cut her off again, but this time it was gentler than before, "Please, my friend in college interpreted my dreams once, and it turned out that what she'd said had been true. I don't know. It's just that...something tells me that I'll get more answers this way."

Catherine sighed and took a few extra seconds before responding, "I hope so."

There was kindness and understanding in her tone that made him think that maybe she was finally starting to believe him. As they sat in the car, unexpectedly the question of *was this the right place* floated across his thoughts like a cloud drifting in front of the sun. Whether or not this particular interpreter was the right one was now a moot point, he'd come this far and there would be no turning back.

They looked long at each other before opening their respective doors and stepping out. The walk up the small flight of steps to the front door felt like an eon but passed in the blink of an eye. Once more they exchanged glances, and with a somewhat shaky hand, Peter pressed the doorbell.

When it buzzed, a light came on behind the single circular window positioned at head height. A few seconds later the white lace curtain was pulled back and a pair of bright eyes in a brown face peered out, the lock was released and the door was opened.

"You must be Peter," the tall thin lady smiled—she'd pronounced his name 'peeta'—and stepped back to allow them to enter.

Her hair was braided with extensions and wrapped in a bun on top of her head. She wore some African tribal garb that Peter naturally couldn't identify, and her arms were adorned with more tribal jewellery. The hallway they found themselves in was decorated with what he thought of as African spiritual paraphernalia, and judging from her accent, he had little doubt of her origins.

"Ah, yes. I'm Peter, and this is my wife Catherine."

"I'm Marabelle," she said in her heavy African accent, as she shook hands with the couple. "This way, please."

She turned and led them to a room on the left side of the short corridor. There was a small round table inside with two folding chairs. More chairs were piled against the right wall, and she took one of them and placed it beside its companion, which happened to be directly in front of the window containing the neon crystal ball and placard.

"Please, have a seat," the interpreter indicated as she sat herself in the chair opposite theirs.

When all were sitting, Marabelle reached across the table for Peter's hand. "It is not for palm reading," she said when he didn't immediately oblige. "It is so I can feel your energy as you speak of the dreams you wish to have answers to."

With a last look at his wife, he extended his hand but the interpreter stopped him, "Wait," she took two deep breaths then nodded. When Peter placed his hand in hers, she emitted a slight gasp and he felt her squeeze slightly.

"Begin," she closed her eyes and continued to breathe deeply. "Tell me the first time you had these dreams."

"They began about three nights ago," Peter said.

He went on to tell her about the ruined landscape that he somehow felt was earth. About the man-crabs and nearly destroyed courtyard. As he spoke, the depth of her breathing increased.

Peter then told her about the second dream and once again being on the hill in that burned landscape. He spoke about being chased by the things again and the same courtyard, but this time finding the underground bone catacombs and the five pillars.

When he began to talk about his most recent dream, a slight vibration ran through the dream interpreter's hand as though a switch had been turned on. He ignored it and continued to relay his ordeal in the boned tunnels, the pillars and the creatures inhabiting them—the four ethereal and the one real—the chase, and the ominous threat. At that moment her breathing shuddered, she released his hand, and her eyes sprang open.

"You have been marked Peter Gentrick."

The words were cryptic.

He looked from Marabelle to his wife and saw the shock in her eyes. This was not what he'd expected. He'd come looking for the meaning of his dreams in hopes that it would provide answers about his missing hours, not to be told that he was part of some *prophecy*. The expression on Catherine's face seemed to echo his sentiment.

"I feel it in you," the interpreter replied after he'd returned his attention to her.

"What? What are you talking about? I came here lo—"

She didn't allow him to finish, rather, she gently completed his sentence for him, "looking for answers to a missing piece of your life. You want that hole in your memory filled."

Shock coursed through him as well and he had to place his hands on the table as much to steady them as to make sure that he didn't fall from his chair. Peter thought back to his call and couldn't remember telling her about his missing memory. He'd simply told her that he'd wanted some dreams interpreted.

Possibly sensing his discomfort, Catherine placed her hand on his thigh, causing him to nearly jump from the chair.

"How...how..."

"How did I know?" Marabelle completed for him again. "There are few of us with the gift. You were right to have your scepticism. Not that dream interpretation is a gift, it's more of a study in psychology, but to truly see inside someone...read their energy and purpose...*that*...is the gift."

"I cannot tell you who marked you or why. That is...*hidden*...from me, nevertheless I can feel the presence upon you. You are meant to do something, *carry* something."

"What? I don't get it. How can you tell all of that from just my dream? And what is it that I'm supposed to carry?" Peter was finding it as equally difficult to doubt her as to believe her.

Yes, she seemed to know things about him. Then again, she could've Googled his name after he'd gotten off the phone with her. Immediately, he cast aside that supposition as being preposterous. Another almost equally insane idea of her being a computer hacker sprang to mind but also just as quickly was dismissed. No matter how he spun his brain trying to come up with some way of Marabelle knowing so much about him, he had to confess that it was simply impossible. If they'd met somewhere else, it still wouldn't explain how she knew about his missing memory.

In the end, and no matter how uncomfortable it made him feel, Peter had to face the fact that there *was* something going on. Maybe he'd been kidnapped and hypnotised into doing something, though he reminded himself again that he didn't believe in hypnosis.

"So, is there anything you can tell me about my dreams? Do they give any hint of what I'm supposed to do...or supposed to... carry?"

The interpreter shook her head, "No. But what I feel—and I don't know how to explain this—is that you need to resist."

It was another ominous comment.

"Resist?"

"Yes, I do not know what. I just feel that..." she breathed deeply before continuing. "I just feel that more than you can imagine is at stake."

"What? You're scaring me," Catherine suddenly piped in. "C'mon Peter, I think we should leave."

"I'm sorry Mrs. Gentrick, I do not mean to scare you, but in fact something *has* happened to your husband, and I fear that his dreams may be just the beginning."

Catherine reached over to remove Peter's hand from Marabelle's—he'd not realized that she'd grasped it again—but the interpreter wasn't ready to release him yet. His wife pulled but the other woman maintained her grip and held him just as firmly in her gaze.

"Resist," she let go of his hand.

His wife placed it on his chest as though it had been injured and she was administering aid, "Come on let's go."

He heard her words but they seemed meaningless because what the other woman had said continued to echo in his mind.

Resist.

What or who was he supposed to resist? They'd come looking for answers, but instead were leaving with a larger mystery. Maybe he should have called—or at least tried to call—his friend Alison after all, then deal with any aftermath from Catherine.

His head was now buzzing with thoughts and questions, and attempting to focus on one was as impossible as identifying a particular locust among the horde. Peter stood and tried to steady the trembling in his legs. Marabelle continued to look at him in earnest, which added a layer of discomfort to his already frazzled mind. Something in her stare spoke volumes. It was as though she knew a lot more than she'd said.

When his wife tugged on his hand, he resisted for a moment, then reached into his back pocket, removed his wallet, thanked the interpreter and deposited $50 onto the table. The woman didn't even acknowledge that money had exchanged hands. Her eyes remained intent on his, and with effort he managed to tear his gaze from hers.

As he followed Catherine to the door, he could still feel her watching him, but he refused to turn around.

Once inside their car, he looked up and saw Marabelle standing at her front door. Peter fought to look away, which was even more difficult because he saw her mouthing the word *'resist'*, over and over. As he drove away, she walked to the sidewalk and he thought he saw her continue her warning.

They remained silent for the short ride home. His wife release a sigh when he turned onto their street and the sound pulled him back to reality. He steered into their driveway and turned off the car but neither of them motioned to get out. Instead, they remained there in silence. His thoughts continued to be a jumble of images and scenes from his nightmares. Floating somewhere beneath was the repeated word of warning.

Catherine finally spoke, "You don't really believe her do you?"

He turned slowly to her before replying, "At this point...I don't know what to believe."

"Peter, you're not *marked*. You just can't remember what you did a couple of nights ago."

"Then you finally believe me?"

The answer was in her eyes, but she nodded anyway, "Yeah…I…yeah, I believe you,"

"But…how did she know those things about me? How did she know my last name?"

"You obviously told her."

He shook his head, "No, I didn't."

"Are you sure? I mean…maybe you did and just can't remember. I mean…realistically speaking, it's a perfectly natural thing to do when you call to make an appointment."

Even though he was quite certain that he'd not told her, Peter had to acknowledge that his wife might be right, "But what about her knowing about my missing memory?"

"You probably told her about that too."

He shook his head again, "No, I didn't. And I'm positive this time that I didn't."

Catherine started to object, but Peter gently reached for her hand, "No, Catherine, I didn't tell her anything about me missing a night of my life."

"What could it all mean then?" her voice quivered.

After sitting and holding hands in silence for a few moments longer, they climbed out of the car and walked into the house hugging each other.

Peter's phone rang and he fished it out of his pocket. The number was not one that he knew, and thoughts of Marabelle forced their way into his mind. He looked from the device to his wife and back again before hesitantly tapping the answer button and placing the phone to his ear.

"Hello?"

A familiar sounding voice said something that had registered for a brief moment, and just as quickly was forgotten, because out of the corner of his eye, he saw it.

CHAPTER 4

James Mason turned in an attempt to get a better look at the approaching apparition, but it vanished as quickly as it appeared. He shook his head. The sight of Faye torn to shreds was unnerving and made him ask how it was possible for her to be displayed as she was. He found it difficult to believe that her other friends, family and work colleagues could ignore what they were seeing.

His recent confrontation with Maria and Tony had been forgotten, replaced with the uncertainty of his mental stability. He watched as Faye's mother approached the coffin dressed in black, her eyes were swollen and she held a kerchief to her nose. Fresh rivulets started again as she stroked her daughter's hair. James was horrified as her hand passed through the crusted gore that matted Faye's once lovely tresses. He was even more shocked that she ignored the traces of blood on her hand when she pulled it away to make the sign of the crucifix.

Beside himself with disbelief, he started to approach the grieving woman but was stopped by another mourner. He'd never seen him before and assumed him to one of his friend's coworkers. What really caught his attention though, were the man's striking emerald green eyes.

"It's a shame what's happened, isn't it?" the stranger remarked.

James found the smooth resonance of his voice reassuring. "Yeah, it is," he replied numbly.

"It's hard to believe," the newcomer continued, shaking his head, "She came to see me last week."

"Yeah, I see—whoa…what do you mean *came* to see you?"

"Oh, I'm sorry. I was her psychiatrist. I'm Doctor Dillington."

"Okay, I…I see."

"How well did you know Faye?"

"I'd known Faye for quite some time—I'm sorry Doctor, but you say you're a psychiatrist?"

"Yes I am. This is not really professional conduct—discussing a case, I mean—but, I don't think…" he trailed off, motioning toward the coffin.

"Yeah…I still can't believe she's gone."

"She was so young," the doctor replied.

He walked to the open casket and looked down at his former patient. James joined him and together they stood in silence looking at his decimated friend. Repulsion and anger rose once again, and he cast a glance at the doctor to try to gauge his sentiment. Like the other mourners, the psychiatrist seemed not to notice the condition of the body.

"Doctor?" James ventured. "What…" he stopped, afraid of how his question might be interpreted.

It was his first time talking to a therapist, although it wasn't *his* therapist, he still wanted to guard his words. Dillington looked at him and motioned that he should continue.

"Well…this might sound strange, but what…what do you see?"

"I don't understand the question," the doctor answered. "What do you mean?"

James took a deep breath. He looked from the doctor, to his friend and back again. "What do you see when you look at her?" he asked at last.

"I'm still not sure I understand the question, but I see my former patient; a beautiful young lady who is no more."

James stared at Faye and scrubbed his face with his hands. He drew another breath then turned back to the psychiatrist. "Does she look…normal to you? I mean she *is* dead, but does the body look…normal?"

"Well, as normal as any other dead body, I suppose. They never look quite the same as they did in life," the doctor replied. He looked at James for a moment. "Is everything alright?"

"I don't know. Maybe I'm seeing things. Does she…does she look…*whole*…to you?"

Dillington looked down at Faye again then shook his head. "She looks whole…I mean…well, you know what I mean. What do you see?"

"In all honesty…" James hesitated again. "Her body is torn. It looks as though an animal has clawed her to death. You don't… you don't see this? I mean…am I losing my mind?"

"I think you need to come and see me. In fact, I think it's imperative that you do. Again, this is against the code of ethics, but I have something to discuss with you."

James felt the doctor's words like an icy blanket falling upon him. He rubbed his hands on his pants to steady himself and to resist a shudder before he nodded.

"Good. Call my office on Monday and make an appointment, and again...my condolences."

He produced a business card from an inside pocket of his blazer. With a final look at Faye, he turned and departed the mortuary, leaving the mourners to their grief.

* * *

The following Monday morning James called Doctor Dillington's office to make the appointment. There'd been more glimpses of the claw over the previous days, and the only thing that had kept him sane was the thought of visiting the psychiatrist. He was relieved when he was told that the doctor had cleared his calendar and was available to see him immediately.

When he arrived, the usual questionnaire was waived and he was admitted without delay. Once inside, he seated himself in a chair opposite the therapist and ran his fingers through his hair, "Thanks for seeing me on such short notice, Doc."

"My pleasure James," the rich baritone replied.

He didn't waste any time, "You'd also said it was imperative that I come."

"Yes, it is." the doctor took a breath and seemed to arrange his thoughts. "It appears that both you and Faye have—or had, as the case may be—the same affliction."

"What do you mean?"

"I'd found it odd that both of you were seeing the decimated bodies of one of your friends, while others were not. Did she ever talk to you about her trip to Italy with her best friend Nancy? Did you know Nancy, by the way?"

James shook his head.

"Nevertheless, did she tell you about her trip?"

He shook his head again.

"We discussed it, including the abbey where they stayed close to Rome. At the time I'd though the name had sounded familiar, and after the way she'd described the body of her friend, I'd decided to do some research.

"As it turns out, the monks at this abbey are famous for being highly skilled at exorcisms. The Abbot and a Brother Sacchiteli even remembered the two ladies staying the night there. They went on to say that they initially didn't want to allow anyone in since they were conducting an exorcism that very night. But because of the inclement weather and the distance from the city, they'd agreed to let them remain.

"You see, James, with the type of entity they were banishing, it was imperative that there be no other people in the residence."

"I'm lost Doctor Dillington. What does any of this have to do with me?"

"Yes, yes, I'm getting to that. They were saying that the abbey had to be empty of everyone except the two conducting the ritual. But against their better judgment, they allowed Faye and her friend to stay. Anyway, they completed the rite and all would have been well had the girls not gone wandering in the...*place of worship.*"

The doctor paused and took a drink from a glass on the coffee table that James hadn't noticed earlier. He did however note the way the psychiatrist had finished his explanation, but set it aside, convinced that it was his imagination.

Dillington set his glass down and continued. "Unfortunately they ventured into the very room that contained the demon...and released it. Abbot Angelini and Brother Sacchiteli were unaware that the thing had attached itself to one of the girls and eventually killed her."

"Killed her?" James repeated the words almost in a daze. "You…you mean Faye?"

"Yes, eventually Faye, but it killed her friend Nancy first."

"No, I think you're wrong there Doc. Faye had said they couldn't find the cause of Nancy's death."

"That is true. To most, the victims look as though they died of natural causes, however if one can see the true nature of death, then they are…*tagged* by the entity and will be its next victim."

James felt a growing emptiness in the pit of his stomach as though a stopper had been removed, "Are you trying to say that this…thing…*tagged* me? That I'm going to be the next to die?"

"Yes it would appear that you are. Unfortunately, you could see how Faye had been killed. All is not lost though. In order to save yourself, you must go to the Lazio region of Italy. Close to Rome is the Abbey Starita. It is there and only there that you can rid yourself of this curse."

James was flabbergasted.

"Do you understand what I've told you Mr. Mason—James? Do you understand James?"

All he could do was nod repeatedly. A thin film of perspiration broke out on his forehead and before long his shirt was clinging to his body. He tugged at it in hopes of cooling himself, but the moisture kept attracting it back. His mind was scattered. He didn't want to die…especially not like Faye. The thought of being torn to pieces by some unknown demon made his heart stutter.

After another deep breath, he was able to finally find his voice, "Yes…yes…I do. How much time do I have? I mean…how long had Faye been seeing this…thing…before it killed her?"

"It's difficult to say, but with each soul it reaps it grows stronger, so I would recommend that you leave for Italy as soon as possible. If you would like, I could have my secretary make the necessary arrangements for you and we could add the costs onto my bill."

"Huh…um…yeah. Yeah…sure Doc. Um…that'd be fine."

"Are you okay, James? I know that this news is disconcerting, but you must pay attention and act swiftly."

"Yes. Yes, I will Doctor. Thank you."

"One more thing, James, and this is very important. You must not under any circumstances try to concentrate on this apparition."

Unable to hide his shock, he blurted, "Concentrate on it! Fuck no! Sorry."

Dillington raised his hand, "It's quite alright James. I can only imagine the stress you must be under."

Although he was still filled with terror at the thought of being the demon's next victim, he did his best to put on steadier airs, "Thanks Doc. But like I said, I have no intention of concentrating on this thing. I just want it gone."

The doctor studied him for a moment as though he fought some inner battle of his own, "That's good to hear James. You see… in some ways, I feel responsible for Faye's death."

"How could you be responsible? This demon thing killed her."

"Yes, that's true. But when she came to see me, I'd not truly believed that what she'd told me had been real, so in my ignorance and arrogance, I had told her to concentrate on it to prove to herself that it was just a figment of her imagination. But now that I know it *is* real, I want to try to redeem my earlier and very costly mistake."

"It's okay, Doc…well…you know what I mean. If Faye had told me what she'd been seeing, I wouldn't have believed her either. I wonder…"

"Go on," the psychiatrist urged when he wouldn't finish.

James was contemplative for some time as visions of his friend and their weekend getaway flashed through his mind, "Well…it's just that we had taken a camping trip to Diamond Beach a few weeks ago, and Faye had been acting a little weird. At one point in the car, she'd blurted something out. Something like…asking us if we'd seen something. I remember that I'd made fun of her," he gave a rueful chuckle, "Now…if I'd only known."

The doctor was sympathetic, "There would have been nothing that you could have done, James. By that time, the demon probably had a firm hold on her. But it might not be too late for you if you act quickly, and for your own sake you must never forget what I've told you about not concentrating on this thing."

"Thanks Doctor Dillington. I still feel a little guilty for the way I'd treated her that day, but I'll take your advice."

"You're welcome. But also remember that although concentrating on it is fatal, I still don't know enough about this entity to guarantee that you will be safe even if you don't."

The slight confidence that had been slowly inflating was suddenly popped by the reality of the statement, "Yeah…I'll remember."

"Very well, I'll have my secretary Lauren make the necessary arrangements and notify you," Dillington rose to usher him out.

James stopped at the door when he felt a hand on his shoulder and heard the psychiatrist's voice in his ear. He turned and found himself looking into those brilliant green eyes, the whites of which seemed vibrant and aglow as though with an inner light. The sight seemed odd, but he surmised that it was his frazzled mind playing tricks on him. It had to be his preoccupation with the possibility of his impending death that was causing him to obviously not think clearly. Soon however, it would be over, he would be in Italy being rid of this demon and getting his life back to normal. He just hoped that he could maintain his sanity until then.

"Good luck James, and *Godspeed*," Dillington smiled.

All he could do was smile back and nod as he hurried from the office.

* * *

Two days after his visit to the psychiatrist, James found himself on an Alitalia flight heading to Leonardo Da Vinci International Airport in Italy. He'd repeated glimpses of the clawed appendage but knowing the danger involved, he'd used all of his willpower to avoid trying to get a better look. It was especially nerve-wracking because he didn't know at which point the entity might decide to kill him. One thing was certain though, if it didn't kill him by tearing him apart, it would with the anxiety and stress it was causing.

When the plane landed after a seeming lifetime in flight, he'd a minor sense of relief. It also appeared that the doctor had gone farther than he'd expected, because when he finally cleared customs and stepped out of the airport into the predawn light, there was a car with a potbellied, balding driver holding up a sign with his name written in bold letters.

"I'm James Mason," he said, approaching the driver.

"Mr. Mason," the chauffeur replied in heavily accented English. "Doctor Dillington sent me to pick you up. Eh...I'm Angelo Sandista," he extended his hand.

"You know where we have to go?" James inquired as they

shook.

"Si, si. Eh...we go to the Abbey Starita...si?" the man replied nodding.

"Si—um, yes."

"Good, good. You get in, I'll get your bag," he held the rear door opened for him.

James climbed into the vehicle and Angelo closed the door then placed his duffel bag into the trunk. Within moments he was back behind the wheel and they pulled away from the curb to merge with the departing traffic.

Italy had been a destination he'd planned on visiting sometime, but it had never been tops on his list. Had it not been for his current predicament, he might have been marvelling at the old-styled buildings they were passing, and snapping one or two photos. At the moment however that was the furthest thing from his mind. The only thing he could really think about was getting to the abbey and getting cured.

His driver tried to engage him in conversation, but with an end to his dilemma in sight, and the surrealism of the situation, he was only able to provide one word responses. Angelo eventually stopped trying, and continued on in silence.

When they arrived at their destination, James didn't wait for him to open the door. Instead he was out of the car the instant it stopped as though the vehicle were on fire, and making his way to the trunk to get his bag.

After the sedan pulled away in a cloud of dust and disappeared back the way it had come, James Mason found himself bag in hand, and standing on a circular driveway looking at the origin of his recent misery. It was a non-threatening looking place with a gravel walkway leading from the arc of the drive to the protruding entrance. The building itself stretched out on either side of the access and ended a few feet from high hedges that enclosed the grounds.

Out of the corner of his eye he caught another glimpse of the claw, and again he fought the natural instinct to try to get a better look. This time however, the apparition lingered longer than usual and when he finally decide to look, it quickly withdrew.

An eerie chill snaked through him. He shuddered and tried to steady his nerves as visions of Faye lying torn apart in her coffin came flooding back. James assured himself that wouldn't be his fate, but a second appearance of the entity so quickly, dispelled his courage like vapours blown in the wind, and caused him to take flight toward the building.

He began shouting and pounding on the door, completely oblivious of the brass knocker that bumped from the force of his blows. It seemed like he'd been hammering for hours before a sheepish looking monk answered.

"You gotta help me!" he was nearly in tears.

The clearly mystified brother stood staring at the apparent madman, "Non parlo inglese. Che cosa volete?"

"English? Do you speak English?" James yelled when he thought he recognized the word. Not waiting to be invited into the building, he forced his way past the monk.

The other man circled back around him and retreated several steps with a look of fright on his once puzzled face, "Non capisco cosa stai dicendo. Aspetta, ti farò avere qualcuno che parla inglese," the monk said as he turned on his heels and disappeared around the left corner.

James hesitated for a moment. He was in a strange place and not sure if his request had been understood. The sudden thought that the holy man might have left him there so that he could reach a telephone and summon the authorities occurred to him. If they arrived and took him away before he could somehow explain his reason for barging into the monastery, it could spell his doom. Who knows how long he would be kept in jail before being allowed to leave. Further, it was unlikely that they would even believe him. Before these recent incidents, he would've had a difficult time believing it himself.

His thoughts turned to the weekend trip to Diamond Beach and the way he'd mocked Faye in the car. He couldn't risk that happening to him with his life hanging in the balance. James knew that his only hope for survival was to convince these men that he was in dire need. The decision was an easy one, he had to give pursuit, had to stop that imagined phone call.

"Where are you going? Come back here!" he yelled and took off in the direction the brother had taken.

He turned the corner and saw the tail of the man's robes round a curve in the hall. Undaunted, James pounded after him and was a little surprised at how fast the monk could move wearing sandals.

When next he saw him, he was entering a set of large double doors. Without thought as to what could lie beyond, he hastened after the fleeing figure and found himself in what appeared to be the main eating area for the brothers. Countless long tables and benches filled this huge room in perfect rows that led to a slightly raised platform where another long table sat perpendicular to the others. There was a large crucifix erected nearly to the vaulted ceiling and centred in front of a stained glass window. His quarry was quickly approaching that platform.

James paused for a moment when he saw that each of the

tables was filled to capacity with the brothers of the order. They turned as one to observe the new arrival and a palpable hush filled the room.

The sighting came again to his periphery, and this time he couldn't hold back the tears. His fear heightened to a maddening rush, his heart hammered at his breast and images of his friend torn to pieces flashed into his memory like fireworks exploding in the night. Without conscious effort his legs propelled him through the room to the platform as all eyes trailed after him. He could hardly form the words as tears mingled with saliva dripped down his chin.

Finally he was able to calm himself enough to speak, "Please...please, you gotta help me!"

Another approach of the apparition almost made him snap his head around but he resisted. Suddenly he felt something rip into his shoulder sending pain coursing through his body and forcing him to his knees. James put his hand to his shoulder and felt moisture. When he held it up, there was nothing at first, but slowly blood materialized and ran down his forearm to his elbow.

"See! See, it's here! It's here!" he turned his palm outward for the brothers to examine before frantically crawling along the length of the table. "Doctor Dillington told me that you would be able to get rid of this thing. He said...he said that you'd done it before. That you were good at getting rid of demons."

A tall brother with white hair and matching beard rose from the table and came over to place a hand on his shoulder, "Senor, please, calm down. I am Abbot Rugario. What is it that you seek?"

James turned around on his knees and clutched at the Abbot's robe, nearly hugging him around the thighs. "Help me...help me. A while ago you let two girls stay here."

Rugario couldn't hide his surprise, "How do you know of them?"

"One of them...one of them was my friend. They brought something back. It killed them. Now it wants me...it wants me!"

Rugario pulled back a few steps and James crawled after him looking pleadingly up into the other man's face. The Abbot stared down with an expression of comprehension that changed to horror almost instantly.

He turned to the remaining brothers at the table, "Mio Dio. L'Abate Angelini aveva torto. È stato rilasciato. Tutti devono andarsene."

The sound of long benches and tables scarping against the stone floor filled the room as all assembled stood and began to make their way to the exit. Rugario placed a hand on the shoulder of a blonde-haired brother who'd been at the table beside him and was making his way past the kneeling James, "Not you Brother Famuso, I'll need your help."

A perplex expression suddenly appeared on the Abbot's face, and he reached down to feel his robes. He then held his hand up and his eyebrows arched when he saw that it was stained with blood.

"You...you see it, don't you...don't you?" James cried. "It's my blood...it's my blood!"

"Heaven help us, it's almost out. There is no time for an evacuation. We must rid him and ourselves of this thing immediately."

He signalled to some of the other men to help James to his feet, and together they all hurried from the eatery.

A few moments later—but for James Mason it seemed a

never-ending trek—they arrived in a large room filled with flickering light. Etched into the floor was an eye within a triangle within a circle. At the points of the triangle, as well as at the corners of the eye, black oil lanterns stood on holders driven into the floor. A larger circle of white lanterns surrounded this formation. James was placed in the centre of the eye, while the brothers formed a circle outside of the ring.

Abbot Rugario stepped away from his flock and stood before him at the top of the triangle. In his hand he held a marble carving of a four-legged creature hunched over. The thing had its head reared and one clawed hand raised in an attack. Additional spikes lined its back and the forked tail that was curled around its body contained hooks.

He offered the carving as if for inspection, "We know what afflicts you and can rid you of it, but you must do exactly as I say. Do you understand?"

Even though the accent was thick, he was able to comprehend what was said. The sight of the object of his torment caused him to flinch slightly.

Rugario continued, "The visions are coming faster, are they not?"

James didn't trust his voice to hold. Fear, misery, and despair swirled within him like debris in a tornado, one constantly overtaking another in repeated rotation, so that he nearly collapsed in resignation. Finally doing his best to subdue his inner turmoil, he nodded.

"This is what you are seeing, is it not?" the Abbot said more as an affirmation than an inquiry.

James nodded again.

"When I tell you, I want you to concentrate on bringing the

beast forward. Once it is out in the open, we will imprison it." Rugario took another step forward and placed a hand on James' shoulder, "Be brave, son, be brave."

He then turned and addressed his brethren in Italian. "You all know what is required of you, the risks and the sacrifice. Would that it could be otherwise...but unfortunately..."

One or two of the assembly shifted slightly, but the rest seemed steadfast and resolute. At a signal from the Abbot, they began a prayer.

Instantly James felt claws climb up his back, but unlike in the cafeteria, the thing didn't seem intent on attacking him. Rather, it appeared to be experiencing either anxiety or excitement. When it perched on his right shoulder, his first impulse was to quickly turn to have a better look, however a momentary twinge of fear stayed his head.

The Abbot signalled to his assembly again and their prayer changed, sending the creature into a frenzy running back and forth across his upper back. At last it settled on his left shoulder and he could slightly distinguish its horrific countenance from his periphery. Though it was ethereal, he could clearly see fangs larger and sharper than its talons lining the upper and lower jaws of its protruding mouth. Saliva dripped onto his shirt as the thing snapped its maw open and close.

James closed his eyes, shuddered, and took a few steps closer to the lantern at his back. When he opened his eyes again, Rugario was signalling to him that he was to begin. Taking a deep breath, he closed his eyes once more and envisioned himself taking hold of the beast and dragging it in front of him. He reopened them and turned to the creature, willing it to remain and solidify onto this plane.

The thing walked across his chest, brought its mandible to his chin and licked at the fear-induced sweat covering his face with its black, forked tongue. Oozing boils dotting the surface, and an odour akin to decay emanated from it.

James shuddered again and called upon his entire resolve to remain motionless as he'd been instructed. Looking through the fairy creature, he could see the Abbot closing in with his arm extended, grasping the grotesquely carved image of the beast.

A pinprick of light emerged from the figurine and blossomed outward like a slowly expanding star. It grew in intensity until it nearly eradicated the torment upon his chest and he began to close his eyes to prevent himself from being blinded.

"No!" Rugario shouted, "You must continue to hold the beast in your gaze else it will find escape!"

James nodded and squinted against the blinding iridescence. By now Rugario stood within arm's reach of him, the carving still in his hand and the demon still perched upon his chest. The body of the thing began to stretch and fade towards the idol, and immediately it latched onto him, temporarily gaining purchase but continuing to elongate and dissolve.

It opened its mouth as though it was going to clamp its fangs onto his face, but instead the creature spoke, "Maldoba!"

There was a blinding flash and James' world was plunged into darkness. Behind his sightless eyes he could still see the imprint of the light from the sculpture, and the silhouette of the beast as it was being imprisoned.

The demon would not let him go so easily though, for it leaped at him one last time causing him to stumble blindly backwards and knock over the lantern. He felt heat as fire flowed with the running oil and bodies began to bump into him in the confusion that ensued.

James stumbled about the room in his blinded state coughing from the smoke and alternating between colliding with the frantic monks and knocking over more and more lanterns. A cacophony of screams and cries reached his ears. Some were gargled as though something was forcibly silencing the terrified men.

He didn't know where in the room he'd been knocked to, and without his sight he wasn't sure that he'd be able to escape the blaze. Occasionally, warm liquid splashed onto him as he continued his mad grope. The heat began to become oppressive and he smelled an odor that he instinctively associated with burning flesh, though he'd never smelled it before.

He wanted to put his hands over his ears to drown out the wails of the brothers but knew that he needed them as his antennae if he hoped to find the door and safety.

His prospects of escape were suddenly dashed when he was unexpectedly knocked to the ground by the continued crush of the distraught men. With the thickening smoke and increasing heat, breathing became difficult. The last things he heard before he slipped into oblivion were the screams of the brothers as they were engulfed in the blaze.

* * *

It took the firefighters nearly six hours to squelch the inferno, but at last it was beaten. By that time there was nearly nothing left of the abbey fully standing except for a couple of the outer walls. Here and there tendrils of smoke could still be seen gyrating in the breeze, but there was little possibility of the blaze erupting again through the many puddles of blackened water and soaked wood.

As fire investigator Luca Gigliano carefully picked his way through the charred rubble, the aroma of scorched flesh permeated his immediate surroundings. It was an odour he'd never quite become accustomed to and was certain that he never would. To do so would mean that he'd been desensitized to the horrible aspect of death by fire, and to him that would minimize the loss of life.

He also knew he should wait for the others so they could examine the rubble together, but something compelled him. Besides, with the firemen now distancing themselves from the ruins so his team could do their work, he saw no reason to delay any longer.

Naturally, it would have been much easier to lift the fallen roof from the bodies with the help of his partner Giamo—who at the moment was working at the other side of the building—but he was driven to release these men of God from their seared prison, if only temporarily.

The first piece of stone he grasped was a little larger that his upper body and his attempts to move it resulted in his palms being scrapped raw. He did however catch a glimpse of one of the brothers before the slab slipped from his grip to teeter back onto the body. The corpse was neither charred nor blistered and had blood oozing from a slash in its throat. Confused but unperturbed, he looked around and spotted an iron rod that he could use to pry the hunk of marble from the cadaver.

A little effort saw it lifted and cast aside to reveal the mangled form that he'd first spied beneath. It was immediately apparent that this victim did not die from the fire. There were obvious signs of severe trauma and the victim appeared to have been mauled by a wild animal. He was further puzzled when he noticed the arm of another of the monks lying close by, as it too appeared to have suffered the same damage.

As he continued to survey the wreckage, he noticed different appendages protruding from beneath the brick and mortar.

"It's a shame what's happened, isn't it?"

A rich baritone startled him from his examination. The man seemed to have materialized from thin air. He looked to be in his late twenties or early thirties, and was well manicured. Luca was nearly mesmerized by his brilliant green eyes that seemed to glow with a light of their own.

"What? How did—"

"It's a terrible shame when such things happen to *men of God*." the stranger interrupted with a shake of his head.

"Wh—yes..." Luca stammered.

"They'll get their reward for what they've done here." the man continued as he turned and walked away.

Luca stared mystified at his departing back, then, out of the corner of his eye, he saw them.

CHAPTER 5

Doctor Ethan Dillington looked into the mirror over his bathroom sink and smiled as he washed his hands. He was still not completely accustomed to the vibrant green of his eyes—which were one of the many gifts from Mobious. All he had to do was send a few souls to his benefactor and he would continue to be rewarded. Some might consider what he did to be evil, but then again, there were people in the world far more sinister, and they were living a privileged life, so why couldn't he.

He'd just returned from Italy—if it could be termed as such. His new abilities allowed him to do many things, accomplish many feats, including out of body travel. His smile widened as he recalled the look on Luca's face when he'd made himself known. Dillington had thought the man had actually shat himself from the way he'd jumped. If he hadn't then, he surely would soon when Mobious began to make his presence felt more and more. And when the demon eventually took *his* soul—as it did with every other—both of their powers would increase.

Thoughts of that annoying detective Mugabba began to creep into his mind like probing cockroaches, but he forced them away. There would be plenty of time to deal with that minor frustration later. Instead, he mused about how he'd never really believed in heaven or hell and praised his luck for having stumbled across his new *friend* completely by accident. Memories of the fateful day began to surface and replace the troublesome lawman, causing his smile to increase even more.

* * *

It'd been five days since his grandmother's funeral and he'd finally gotten around to visiting the house. The smell of 'old people' still lingered throughout the two-story home, and he was reminded of why he'd never really visited her while she'd been alive.

He moved from room to room in search of some hidden treasure, refusing to accept the realization that there would be nothing to be had. If the pervasive odour could be harvested and sold then he would be able to earn a fortune.

His search eventually landed him in the attic—which didn't smell much better but he was able to attribute the unpleasantness to the mounds of dust and mildew that coated its contents. As he looked about the confined space, he noted with disappointment that there truly was nothing of significant value to be had. All that he could see was an old-style floor mirror, a dressmaker's mannequin, and an odd assortment of boxes and cartons—none of which offered much hope.

Determination got the better of him however, and after rummaging through the mix, he noticed a gray pad-locked metal box. His spirits lifted as he thought that his luck may in fact have changed. Thinking that it contained something worthwhile or that he could easily sell, Ethan decided to take it for himself so that the rest of his extended family wouldn't be able to lay claim to whatever it was.

As there was nothing of interest left, he took his discreet leave of the home, with the hopes that none would be the wiser.

* * *

Dillington scrubbed his face with foam as the memories flowed back to him like returning waves to a beach.

* * *

Ethan walked into his apartment and set the locked box down on the coffee table in his small living room. Seeing that he naturally didn't have the key, he found a screwdriver and inserted it under the lid. After some effort and slippage, he was able to pry it open.

A brown leather-bound journal and a smaller cube-shaped box made of wood stared back at him. He lifted the miniature case and felt a sudden and curious surge of energy tingle through his body. The skin on his arms rippled with goose bumps but Ethan dismissed it as having been caused by a draft of cool air from somewhere.

After restoring the box to its original place, he picked up the book. It was a little heavy and seemed old, though the binding held together well. The pages were rough as though they'd been fashioned by hand, and a faint musty odour emanated from the slightly yellowed sheets. The ink was faded and the handwriting was of beautiful calligraphy, leaving no doubt that it was very old text.

He began to read.

'If you are reading this then you have assumed a most pre-eminent undertaking. This is something that is not to be taken lightly, for entrusted to you is the safety of humankind. For generations, the women of our line have been the keepers of a horror beyond imagining. The idol you have been given is the prison of the demon, Mobious the Corruptor.

'You must keep its safeguarding a secret. The knowledge of its existence is only to be revealed upon passing on the burden. And it must be passed only to your female lineage. For reasons unknown, the creature lays dormant at the caress of a woman's hand, but a man's

touch wakens the beast.

'Few men have ever been able to resist the temptations of Mobious. Thus far, only the brothers at the Abby Starita have denied the creature, but even they feared that members of later generations would not. Therefore they have entrusted it to our line, and now it is being entrusted to you.

Keep it safe for now and forever, lest everyone and everything you love and hold dear be destroyed.'

The remainder of the journal was blank, so he closed it and replaced it to its original position in the box. His heart and mind raced and he didn't know if it was from what he'd just read or the power he still felt coursing through him from touching the smaller container.

He picked it up again and felt the same surge anew. Unexpectedly a voice entered his mind. It sounded like a whispered growl and he looked around startled.

"Release me."

"What?" Ethan asked aloud.

"Release me," the voice said again.

"What—who?"

"Release me and your rewards shall be great."

Immediately, visions began to flash through his mind like a video collage on a wall screen. He was entranced and enraptured. Dillington saw himself surrounded by wealth, luxury and women. Something told him that they were more than just his imagination, somehow—and he couldn't say how—he knew that what he was looking at were glimpses of his promised future.

"Release me, and all this shall be yours."

"How do I do that?" he asked somewhat excitedly.

"Open the box and remove my prison."

Ethan reached into the metal container on the table and felt the power surge yet again at handling the smaller cube. When he slid the lid open he found a marble carving of a four-legged creature hunched over. It was unlike any animal he'd ever seen. The thing had its head reared with one talon raised and seemed to snarl at him. He could see additional spikes lining its back and a hooked forked tail curled around its body.

Dillington held the figurine up for a closer inspection, "Is this you?"

"Yes."

"So, how do I free you?"

"You must give me to another."

"And that's all?"

"We must convince them to take me to the Abbey Starita. The same rite that imprisoned me can also set me free."

"That's it?"

"No. Another must also go there at the same time to bring me back."

"How am I going to convince these people to do all of this?"

"I have given you the power. Behold yourself in the looking glass."

Confused but curious, Dillington went to his bathroom to see himself in the mirror. The face looking back at him opened its mouth in disbelief at the vibrant green eyes that had replaced his brown ones. Those same eyes alternated from looking at the reflection to looking at the idol in his hand and back again. Wonder, fear and dark excitement were intertwined in them and his mind tried to make sense of what had happened.

"How did you do that?" he asked when he could think clearly enough to speak.

"That is not your only gift. I have also granted you the power of

persuasion, and as my strength increases so too shall your rewards."

* * *

The doctor pulled one of the monogrammed cashmere towels that hung from a rack beside the sink and started to dry his hands. He looked at himself in the mirror again and couldn't resist smiling at his turn of fortune. The reflection of the other towel with its matching 'R.H' initials caused a chuckle to escape him.

That's something else I'll have to change in the near future, he thought to himself.

Outside of his opulent high-rise condominium, he could hear a storm brewing as intensifying winds and thunder overtook the skies and seemed to herald destruction. For a brief moment he wondered if it was another of Mobious' handiworks, but quickly dismissed the idea as he replaced the towel and reached for his toothbrush. His mind was awhirl with thoughts of the creatures' promises and his green eyes glowed as he replayed the events that had brought him to his glory.

* * *

Ethan answered the door on the second knock and was greeted by the surprised but smiling face of Peter Gentrick. Two days after finding the box, he'd invited him over for drinks and to watch the hockey game on TV.

He admitted his friend into his less than spacious home and ushered him to the living room before going to the kitchen himself. When he returned he'd two bottles of beer gripped in his right fist, and offered one to his guest. The two men then sat themselves upon the couch with beer in hand, waiting for the puck to drop.

Peter looked at his host, "You know Ethan, I can't get over your coloured contacts."

"Thanks, I just wanted a change," he replied

"Funny thing is, I didn't know you wore glasses...or are those just for fashion?"

"Ya got me," Dillington conceded. "Actually Peter, there's another reason I asked you to come over tonight. I've got something I'd like you to take a look at."

His friend smiled, "Sure thing."

Ethan set his bottle down and reached under the coffee table. There was no need to look because he knew exactly where it would be. His fingers grasped the lockbox easily and, lifting it out, he set it down besides his beer. His excitement was electric; the beating of his heart nearly palpable against background noise of the TV. He could barely contain himself as he opened the lid, reached inside and pulled out the small cube. Mobius' energy surged through him once again.

Finally, his green eyes found Peter's "You're not going to believe this."

"What is it?"

He opened the small container and smiled as he placed the sculpture into Peter's hand. From his minute shudder, it was apparent that his friend felt the same sensation he had from holding the statue. Instantly, Ethan could hear the other man's thoughts as though they were being broadcasted through a loudspeaker.

"What the fuck is this piece of crap?" Peter suddenly gasped and quickly turned his head to the right, "What the...?"

Mobious' voice pushed through his connection, disrupting the other man's thoughts and replacing them with his own loud, clear and ominous commands. "Now, use the power I have given you to send him to The Abbey."

"How?"

"Did you say something?" Peter asked.

Ethan shook his head and tried to concentrate on the voice only he could hear.

"The power to control him is in your eyes. Focus on his thoughts."

Nodding, Dillington steadied his mind and sought Peter's. Not wanting to risk breaking his concentration, he reached out and grasped his friend's hand causing him to turn to face him. The instant their eyes met he began to exert his will.

What happened next was so instantaneous that it caught him by surprise. Gentrick was staring wide-eyed at him and in their reflection he could see an emerald glow.

"Peter?"

"Huh," the answer was sluggish.

"I want you to do something for me. Will you do it?"

"Yes...sure...anything."

"I want you to take this carving to the Abbey Starita. Will you do that Peter?"

"Yes," he answered in the same drowsy tone.

"Good Peter, good. You will tell them that you need to have them perform the rite to cleanse you of this evil."

"Yes, cleanse me of evil."

"Excellent Peter. When you hear the word 'Mobious', you will book the next possible flight for Italy, to the abbey close to Rome. Do you understand?"

"Yes."

"You will remember only that you watched the hockey game tonight at a bar."

* * *

A bolt of lightning tore through Ethan's recollection. The minty taste of toothpaste caused him to nearly gag so he spat it into the sink and reached for a glass of water to rinse. After he'd finished, he looked in the mirror once more with approval and pleasure at his brilliant green eyes.

Indeed he had much to smile about, Mobious had been freed and since he'd kept his promises so far, Dillington looked forward to many more rewards.

Turning off the bathroom light, he made his way down the long hallway to his sunken living room, and stood in front of his balcony doors. The spectacular view he commanded of the city from nearly every room of his penthouse suite made him feel like a God looking down upon creation. Though his outer walls were made entirely of glass, there was no concern for privacy because he occupied the tallest building in the area. Plus if he chose, he could close whichever curtains were needed at any given time.

Another forked bolt lit up the night and a strong wind lashed the sides of his home. Thunder boomed and cracked, but that hardly concerned him. Ethan Dillington was so completely filled with rapture at his good fortune that he stretched his arms out wide and turned around and around chuckling to himself. Finally he stopped, placed his hands on his hips and looked out at the darkened sky hovering above city.

Overly satisfied, he walked to his leather couch, threw himself onto it and reached for the remote to turn on the wall-sized television. The picture focused and he gasped when he saw that the news reporter looked almost identical to the red head Nancy he'd sent to Italy to retrieve Mobious. A part of him wished he'd fucked her first—or for that matter, both of them—but at the time it had been the farthest thing from his mind.

Sinking deeper into the soft leather, he allowed himself to recall the night the two young ladies had visited his old apartment.

* * *

The striking redhead, Nancy was the first to enter when he opened the door. Ethan had met her and her friend at a downtown nightclub a few days prior. She had a minute splash of freckles on her nose and cheeks and shoulder-length wavy hair that shone in the florescent light of the outside hallway. He also noticed that her gray eyes seemed to sparkle, and even though he found her attractive, he wasn't attracted to her in particular. She was too tall for his liking, albeit she was thin, but he'd always preferred short, petite women.

Her friend Faye was a little better; being slightly shorter, but she was still a little too tall for his preference. She was however a very pretty 'girl-next-door' type with brown eyes and long brown hair. He had at one point in time liked that kind of girl but now his taste ran to the more exotic and to a certain extent, slutty.

Dillington took their coats but didn't know why because from the moment he'd opened the door for them he'd begun exerting his newly given power. His schoolboy shyness must have taken over and made him treat them with courtesy even though they wouldn't remember much of the night.

When they were both seated he began the second phase of the plan. Nancy was the first. He took hold of her hand and turned her to face him, "Nancy," he began. "I want you to do something for me. Will you do it?"

There was no real reason to continue to ask his victims whether or not they would cooperate, because they didn't have a choice. It was just more of that adolescent modesty flowing through.

"Yes," she replied.

"Great. I want you to suggest going to Italy to Faye."

"Yes, go to Italy," Nancy said in a similarly drowsy voice as his other victims.

"What—"

Faye had started to protest but he looked at her and she fell silent. He must have unknowingly released her from his power while focusing on Nancy, but once again she was firmly under his control.

"Thank you," he said, returning his attention to the redhead. "There's something I want you to do when you're there. I want you to go The Abbey Straita close to Rome. Will you go?"

Again it was unnecessary to ask.

"Yes," she said.

"If you hear anything late at night while you're at The Abbey, I want you to search for it."

"Search for it."

"Yes, but you must be very careful. You must not be caught and you must not give up until you have found the source of the sound."

"Find the source of the sound," Nancy repeated after him.

Satisfied, he turned his attention to her friend, "Faye."

"Huh."

"I want you to go with Nancy to Italy. And I want you to recommend staying at The Abbey. Will you do that Faye?"

"Yes, stay at Abbey."

"Thank you Faye, Nancy," he said turning from one to the other. "When you hear the word 'Mobious', I want you both to book first class tickets on the next available flight to Rome."

"Yes," both girls mumbled wearily.

"Oh, and Faye."

"Huh."

"You'll recommend staying at The Abbey because one of your Italian co-workers told you about it."

"Yes," Faye replied.

The last suggestions he gave came to him out of the blue and he thought they added a nice touch.

"When you leave here, you will remember nothing of this conversation or this visit."

Both girls sleepily gave their assent.

* * *

Lightning continued to burst in fiery bolts across the sky while thunder rumbled and rolled, shaking him from his daydream. The redhead on the TV was gone and a dorky-looking weatherman was in the process of telling the viewers about a clear night ahead.

Ethan thought back on that night for another moment and didn't really know why he'd given those particular instructions to the two ladies. In truth, there'd been no need for one to suggest the trip to the other. Simply telling them to go would've been enough. They would have done anything he'd commanded.

The timing of them staying at the abbey had been one of concern for him however. He'd known that they had to be there at the same time as Peter, but he'd been unsure of how that would have been accomplished. His discussion with Mobious wafted back to him.

* * *

"Do not be concerned, I will arrange it so that they will not be refused lodging." the demon answered.

"How will you do that?"

"Already I am feeding off of the one you call Peter and my power is growing. I will create a storm that night so fierce that pity will be given them by...the men of God." Mobious spat the last part as if the phrase had been dipped in bitter herbs.

Ethan was perplexed by the nature and extent of his new friend's powers but chose to limit his show of doubt. "Why do we need to send the two girls? Isn't one enough to carry you back from there?"

"Yes, one is enough, but it is also possible that she will not survive first contact. If that happens and there is no other, I will surely perish."

* * *

The telephone rang, startling him, but the doctor ignored it. *Probably that damn detective*, Ethan thought to himself, *he can leave a message*.

He started aimlessly changing channels on the television. As usual, there was nothing of interest on and he didn't feel like putting in a DVD so he just kept pushing the 'channel up' button as his mind faded back to the day Faye had gone to his office.

Unlike her friend Nancy, she had not tried to focus on Mobious. He'd tried to plant the suggestion from a distance, but had not been successful, obviously she had been stronger willed than her friend. However, he did manage to plant his name and number in her mind when she'd researched psychiatrists online. From there it had been easy to get her to go along, and the drugs he'd recommended to *help her sleep*, had in fact helped to break her resistance.

After her death, Mobious had moved on to James. Ethan's thoughts now wandered back to the morning of their appointment.

* * *

"Are you sure?"

"Yes, it must be done."

"But will burning down The Abbey destroy your prison?"

"Destroying that place may shatter my prison or it may not. Either way, it will ensure that none can confine me again."

"But, how?"

"Because the knowledge will perish with them all."

"Okay, it will be done. He's nearly here, I can feel him."

There was a knock at the door and his secretary admitted his only appointment for the day.

James Mason looked much more haggard than the time Dillington had seen him at the viewing. It was immediately obvious that he was feeling the effects of Mobious' attention. The wavy gelled hair that the psychiatrist had seen on him at the funeral home was now flat and limp, and he seemed to have developed bags under his eyes.

"Thanks for seeing me on such short notice, Doc," he said

"My pleasure, James."

"You'd also said that it was imperative that I come."

"Yes, it is," he paused for a moment, tempted to put him under his control but decided against it. There was no rush, why shouldn't he enjoy the moment. "It appears that both you and Faye have—or had, as the case may be—the same affliction."

"What do you mean?"

"I'd found it odd that both of you were seeing the decimated bodies of your friends, while others were not," Dillington lied. "Did she ever talk to you about her trip to Italy with her best friend Nancy? Did you know Nancy, by the way?"

James shook his head.

"Nevertheless, did she tell you about her trip?"

He shook his head again.

"We discussed it, including the abbey where they stayed close to Rome. At the time I'd though the name had sounded familiar and after the way she'd described the body of her friend, I'd decided to do some research. As it turns out, the monks at this abbey are famous for being highly skilled at exorcisms. The Abbot and a Brother Sacchiteli even remembered the two ladies staying the night there. They went on to say that they initially did not want to allow anyone in since they were conducting an exorcism that very night. But because of the inclem-

ent weather and the distance from the city, they'd agreed to let them remain.

"You see, James, with the type of entity they were banishing, it was imperative that there be no other people in the residence."

"I'm lost, Doctor Dillington. What does any of this have to do with me?"

"Yes, yes, I'm getting to that. They were saying that the Abbey had to be empty of everyone except the two conducting the ritual. But against their better judgment, they allowed Faye and her friend to stay. Anyway, they completed the rite and all would have been well had the girls not gone wandering in the...place of worship."

Ethan displayed a little of his new power and conjured a glass of water onto the table, noting the slightly surprised expression on James' face. Taking a sip, he tried to hide his smile behind the glass.

There was no need to do even that much, because he could make it so that this latest victim wouldn't remember any of these events. Still, a newly found bravado surfaced and he couldn't help showing off. It wouldn't be long before he would finally be on top of the world.

Setting the glass back onto the table, he continued, "Unfortunately they ventured into the very room that contained the demon... and released it. Abbot Angelini and Brother Sacchiteli were unaware that the thing had attached itself to one of the girls and eventually killed her."

"Killed her?" James repeated, seemingly in a daze. "You...you mean Faye?"

"Yes, eventually Faye, but it killed her friend Nancy first."

"No, I think you're wrong there, Doc. Faye had said they couldn't find the cause of Nancy's death."

"That is true. To most, the victims look as though they died of natural causes, however if one can see the true nature of death, then

they are...tagged by the entity and will be its next victim."

"Are you trying to say that this...thing...tagged me? That I'm going to be the next to die?"

"Yes it would appear that you are. Unfortunately, you could see how Faye had been killed. All is not lost though. In order to save yourself, you must go to the Lazio region of Italy. Close to Rome is the Abbey Starita. It is there and only there that you can rid yourself of this curse."

James sat silently for a few moments. When he opened his mouth no words came, his jaw just worked aimlessly, and Ethan smiled inwardly as he savoured his fear.

"Do you understand what I've told you Mr. Mason—James? Do you understand, James?"

He nodded repeatedly and Dillington saw a thin film of perspiration break out on his forehead. Shortly afterward he began tugging at his shirt. "Yes...yes...I do. How much time do I have? I mean...how long had Faye been seeing this…thing…before it killed her?"

"It's difficult to say, but with each soul it reaps it grows stronger, so I would recommend that you leave for Italy as soon as possible. If you would like, I could have my secretary make the necessary arrangements for you and we could add the costs onto my bill."

"Huh…um…yeah. Yeah...sure Doc. Um...that'd be fine."

"Are you okay James? I know that this news is disconcerting, but you must pay attention and act swiftly."

"Yes. Yes I will Doctor. Thank you."

"One more thing, James, and this is very important. You must not under any circumstances try to concentrate on this apparition."

"Concentrate on it! Fuck no! Sorry."

Ethan nearly broke out laughing at this sudden outburst, but managed to resist. Instead he raised his hand, "It's quite alright James.

I can imagine the stress you must be under."

"Thanks Doc. But like I said, I have no intention of concentrating on this thing. I just want it gone."

After waiting for what he thought was an appropriate amount of time to be convincing, Dillington decided to try to further unsettle the soon-to-be dead man, "That's good to hear James. You see...in some ways, I feel responsible for Faye's death."

"How could you be responsible? This demon thing killed her."

"Yes, that's true. But when she came to see me, I'd not truly believed that what she'd told me had been real, so in my ignorance and arrogance, I had told her to concentrate on it to prove to herself that it was just a figment of her imagination. But now that I know it is real, I want to try to redeem my earlier and very costly mistake."

His words seemed to be having the desired effect for a contemplative look came onto James' face, "It's okay, Doc...well...you know what I mean. If Faye had told me what she'd been seeing, I wouldn't have believed her either. I wonder..."

"Go on," he said.

"Well...it's just that we had taken a camping trip to Diamond Beach a few weeks ago, and Faye had been acting a little weird. At one point in the car, she'd blurted something out. Something like...asking us if we'd seen something. I remember that I'd made fun of her," he gave a little chuckle, "Now...if I'd only known."

Feigning sympathy, "There would have been nothing that you could have done, James. By that time, the demon probably had a firm hold on her. But it might not be too late for you if you act quickly, and for your own sake you must never forget what I've told you about not concentrating on this thing."

"Thanks Doctor Dillington. I still feel a little guilty for the way I'd treated her that day, but I'll take your advice."

"You're welcome. But also remember that although concentrating on it is fatal, I still don't know enough about this entity to guarantee that you will be safe even if you don't."

Ethan got another jolt of satisfaction as the slightly confident expression that had been developing on James' face disintegrate like a dust mound in the wind and he swallowed before replying, "Yeah...I'll remember."

As enjoyable as the moments of toying with him had been, it was now time to put the final phase of their plan into motion. Fixing him with a stare, he put him under his power, "James, there's something I want you to do for me. Will you do it?

"Yes, Doc."

"James, I want you to destroy the abbey before they complete the ritual. When they lead you into the sacred room, I want you to place yourself directly in front of a lantern. Do you understand?"

"Yes, in front of lantern." James murmured.

"Good, James. Good. And when Mobious—the demon—is nearly imprisoned, you will see him lunge at you. It's then that I want you to fall back and knock over the lantern. Knock over as many as you can. Do you understand James?"

"Yes, knock over lanterns."

"Good, you'll remember this when you hear the monks singing," Ethan released him. "Very well. I'll have my secretary Lauren make the necessary arrangements and notify you."

He rose to usher him out and placed a hand on James' shoulder. When his latest victim turned to look at him, Ethan noticed the slight look of confusion on his face and realized that he was still holding onto a little of the hypnotic power that caused his eyes to glow.

"Good luck James, and Godspeed."

* * *

Ethan was pulled from his preoccupation when an unusually large bolt lit up the sky. Though startled, he was still beside himself with glee. Everything had been completed and Mobious had been freed and would continue to reward him for his help.

He was tempted to travel transcendentally to visit the man Luca again, but resisted. The surge of power with each new soul was unmistakable, so he would know when Mobious claimed him.

Dillington would have to ask the demon about Peter, and maybe about the brothers he'd claimed at the abbey. The continuous surge of energy when he'd taken their souls had been near euphoric, though unexpected as nothing had been said about it. However, he should have guessed that would have been the ultimate outcome because the brothers would have been able to easily put out the fire, or at least escape it.

Outside, the tempest was increasing. Lightning arched with growing frequency and thunder crashed unending. Ethan Dillington turned to look out of his glass tower as another bolt shot through the dark. It was then that he realized this truly was not a naturally occurring disturbance.

With his new vision he could see something in the darkened clouds. It was akin to his benefactor, albeit larger than he'd imagined, but he passed it off as part of the demon's magic. However, upon closer inspection, others could be seen behind the apparition, and they were quickly approaching his high-rise home.

Ethan tried to fight the uneasy feeling that was descending upon him. *I didn't know about any others,* he thought to himself.

The figures gradually became smaller the closer they came to him but their ethereal form remained and his fear deepened. He took a deep breath, stepped back and waited. There was nowhere he could go, no place he could run to, so he remained where he was and hoped for the best. All the while the torrent raged, but around the demonic horde it seemed to be at its fiercest. The things were hopping nearly on top of one another, each seemingly eager to be the first to reach him. Massive jaws snapped as talons raked at the sky and each other, but none were injured and none slowed their approach.

The doctor continued to stare dumbfounded at the sight of the malignant spirits, his mouth worked soundlessly and sweat broke out on his brow. The creatures licked at their maws with black, oozing tongues. He attempted to use his mind-reading abilities to determine their intent but was unsuccessful.

Before he knew what was happening, the walls of the penthouse imploded, sending shards and splinters of glass everywhere. The force knocked him over as if he were a fly in a wind tunnel; small and insignificant. He felt himself pinned to the floor unable to move.

Lightning continued to crash, striking his home and plunging the condo into darkness. With each subsequent flash, Ethan and the creatures were silhouetted against the inner wall, their confrontation captured in shadows.

Surprisingly, the encounter ended as quickly as it had begun, and light returned to the unit. Dillington rose from the ground and dusted fragments of broken glass from his clothing and hair. He calmly reached for the remote, switched the television off and tossed the device back onto the couch. Next, he turned off the lights, returning the room to blackness. Lightning flashed, continuing to illuminate the room, and casted a contoured shadow onto the wall.

The outline however, was not that of a man, but of a beast with an elongated head and massive fangs lining it's upper and lower jaws.

www.ingramcontent.com/pod-product-compliance
Lightning Source LLC
LaVergne TN
LVHW031301150826
845672LV00009B/2575

* 9 7 9 8 5 7 4 7 3 7 1 4 9 *